AF674229

Love In Crazy Times

KV Gautam

DIAMOND BOOKS

SMS New Book at 9911044500 for Alert

ISBN : 978-93-5083-094-9

Publisher : **Diamond Pocket Books (P) Ltd.**
X-30, Okhla Industrial Area, Phase-II
New Delhi-110020
Phone : 011-40712100, 41611861
Fax : 011-41611866
E-mail : sales@dpb.in
Website : www.diamondbook.in
Edition : 2012
Printed by : G. S. Enterprises

Love In Crazy Times
By - *KV Gautam*

All characters in this book are fictitious, and any resemblance to real persons, living or dead, is coincidental.

Dedicated to the legendary cartoonist R.K. Laxman, my childhood hero

Acknowledgement

My sincere thanks to the following people:

My friend Rahul Bajpai, for reading the first draft of the book and for giving his honest feedback.

Nisha, for making me understand women better.

My parents Chandrakant Mishra and Sunita Mishra, for bearing up with my different ways.

My Facebook friends, for encouraging me to write the book.

Heartbreak

It was a black day for me. My world had come crushing down. The initial relief of getting rid of a non-working relationship gave way to the realization that I would spend the rest of my life without meeting Purnima. I didn't expect her to ditch me like that.

The moment I reached house I opened a whisky bottle and poured into my glass. In one go, I emptied the glass. My mind was restless. I decided to skip the dinner and sat on the bed with another drink. I kept drinking until fell down on the bed. I rose to lock the door and then fell down on the bed. Thoughts of Purnima kept flooding my mind. I realized my pillow was getting wet under flow of my tears. The night was spent turning sleepless in the bed.

When I opened my eyes in the morning my head was heavy and reeling. I was surprised to see that the world was in its place, very much intact. How come everything was proper in the world when my life had gone for a toss? Anyway, I pushed myself to get ready for the office.

Going to the office made me realize every day that I was working for idiots with inflated egos. I had always dreamt to own a big company of my own some day. I was forced to work under some real jerks just because I didn't have enough money to start my own venture and also because I wanted to get enough work experience before I could take my own path.

At office, I saw the same re-assuring faces who greeted me the same way they did the last day. Our office building, situated at Mohan Cooperative Industrial Estate on Mathura Road, was large and impressive, made with red bricks and glass.

"Good morning," Priya, my colleague, greeted me. I did not feel like replying.

"Hey Amit, what's the matter? You seem to be upset?" She asked turning towards me. She guessed I was feeling down.

"No, nothing," I said giving a feeble smile.

I didn't feel like talking to anyone. I spent the day behaving like a lifeless machine. Suraj, my colleague cum friend, was absent that day. He understands me more than anyone else. May be he is also an oddball like me. We have worked together in two companies. It was our third job together.

While coming back to the home, Purnima's face seemed to be running in my mind. I had wasted five months after this girl and it's been a bitter experience.

Purnima was a typical Delhi girl belonging to a traditional middle class family. I liked her beautiful eyes and dimple in the cheeks. She used to work as graphic designer in the previous company I worked for. We formed friendship and used to go to office together. It's difficult to define whether it was love or just a crush. All I know is that I liked her. She used to make my heart flutter.

It was a love at first sight for me. I still remember the day she had joined the company along with ten other boys and girls. Her tall figure and giggles made her stand out. I used to find excuses to go to the workplace where her team used to sit so that I could have a chat with her in the morning. Later after leaving that company I changed my office-returning route so that I could have her company.

Maybe she always treated me as a friend only. It was me who was having romantic illusions. A week back I had gathered enough courage to propose to her. As I feared, she rejected my advance and since then it was downhill all the way. Finally she broke up with me. My heart, desperate for female attention, mistook her friendly gestures as love. It was all beyond my control.

I was tall and had above-average looks. Her rejection made me feel as if there was something wrong with me. I thought she broke up with me because I didn't look handsome enough, or may be because I didn't belong to a rich family, may be because I didn't have a nice car and a house in Delhi, or maybe I simply didn't understand women. Whatever, it was a blow to my self-esteem.

The next day, Suraj Tripathi came to the office a bit late. He was a lanky boy of 26, born and brought up in Lucknow. He was a knowledgeable person with immense patience. He was also known for his social skills. I had never seen him angry. He was showered with lots of attention by parents as he was their only son. His father had retired from a government job and his mother was a school headmaster. He was quite close to his mother, sharing everything with her, even topics related to girls. This made him both a mama's boy and an emotionally secure young man. He was clean-shaven and always dressed in white shirt and dark-coloured pants in the office, following dictates of Romila about formal attire. Brought up in a middle class family, he had a strong sense of morality.

"Hello," he exclaimed on seeing me. I didn't understand why he was so happy when I felt down. I was feeling like hell. I replied to his greetings nevertheless.

"She broke up with me," I said in a low tone, when he sat on his seat. His desk was close to my desk.

"I knew it would happen one day. Forget about her. She was elder to you any way," he said. I had told him that Purnima was two years older to me.

"It has nothing to do with age," I said philosophically.

"Hey, it's real life. Don't behave like a film character," he said sarcastically, and added "in any case she didn't love you."

"How can you say so?" I asked. I was surprised how he came to know about this secret.

"A male friend does not always translate into a boyfriend in Delhi, my dear friend. She was just a friend of yours," he said deadpan. It hurt, especially because it was true.

"You don't understand girls," he said adding salt to the injury.

"You may be right," I said with a sad tone. Then we proceeded to work by focusing on the monitors of our desktops.

May be Suraj was right. Being born in and having spent first nineteen years of my life in a non-happening place Gorakhpur and having an over-protected childhood, I didn't get much opportunity to interact with the opposite sex. My mother made sure I didn't have any contact with girls outside of my relations. She feared I would get out of her hand into the lap of a young girl. She wanted to control everyone, me, my two young brothers and even my father. I had not forgiven her for beating me up regularly without any fault of mine in my childhood. I guessed she used to beat kids up just to release her frustrations of everyday life. My father blamed her behaviour on her own painful childhood when she had lost her mother when she was a baby and didn't get love at home, and was married off at a young age. I used to be a shy and calm kid in childhood and I never forgot her bad behaviour nevertheless.

My father was a gentleman who was locally famous for not taking any bribe in his service in the Postal Department. It was remarkable considering every single government employee was largely considered neck-deep in corruption. Even my father used to tell us stories about his colleagues who sold their soul for as little as Rs. 10.

Once my mother caught me talking to a girl of our colony and she created a full-brown drama. She didn't explain why my talking with her was so wrong. Her draconian code of conduct made me keep a lengthy distance from any pretty young thing. Even in college days I hardly got any chance to interact with the opposite sex. There were just couples of girls in the collage who hardly attended classes fearing eve-teasing by collage hooligans. To top it all, there were hardly any classes as professors preferred to give tuition classes for a fee at home. For them salary from the university seemed like an additional income. I felt like a student only during the exam time.

Sexual segregation and raging hormones of the youth were the reason why adult films shown in the morning shows were hugely popular in the town. Watching those sleazy movies were something most of young adults did, but no one wanted to admit. People could enjoy two hours of titillation sitting on the front stalls for just Rs. 5. They were not hardcore porn, though some of the films had clippings of hardcode porn inserted in between the regular scenes by the theater owners. Some of the adult films were more popular than regular Hindi films. I had watched one such adult film out of youthful curiosity. That English film 'Oh Babylon' surprisingly turned out to be a high-brow film, with the story set in the ancient Greece. The only titillating factor in the film was nudity.

A classmate of mine was fond of those morning shows. The worse thing was that even his father was also fond of them. Once, both father and son were watching the same show. On coming out of the cinema hall, they spotted each other, just ignored and went away as soon as possible maintaining a comfortable distance.

Increased nudity and titillation in regular Hindi films now must have taken business away from those morning shows, I thought.

I felt like blaming my small town upbringing for my Purnima fiasco.

For the straight fifth day, I was seeing Purnima's face on the computer screen while working. I didn't feel like working and just kept mulling over what had happened between us. May be it was my fault that I mistook her friendly gestures to be love. I also repented having spent money on her. For several months we traveled by bus together and I had purchased her ticket so many times. Suddenly it seemed to be a waste of money. I wondered if there was a law, using which I could ask for refund from her. I remembered one day while plying from Ashok Vihar to Paharganj, the bus suddenly stopped mid way and commuters started to run out of the bus in a tearing hurry. Within seconds the bus was empty as commuters pushed and shoved one another to get out of the bus, while the conductor kept instructing everyone to be patient and calm. I saw one man with a cap calmly jump out of the bus through the window. Some people got their clothes torn in the struggle. A woman was shouting "don't pull my sari," while a young boy was asking "where is my sandal?" Soon, only I, Purnima and the conductor were inside the bus.

"What has happened?" I asked the conductor nervously.

"Nothing. Someone has spread the rumour of fire," the conductor replied calmly.

Soon, the passengers realized their folly as there was no trace of the fire in the bus. Again there was a rush and struggle among passengers to get inside and grab seats. Same pushing, shoving and shouting! I saw the capped traveler jump inside through window calmly and grab his seat.

After the last meeting I lost touch with Purnima. A year later I got the news that she was married off. May be she was under parental pressure to go for an arranged marriage. May be romantic love was out of question for her due to a strict upbringing in her conservative family. Maybe she didn't find me attractive enough. I could never estimate the amount of family pressure on her. It's not easy to be a girl in the Indian society. I kept wondering.

The weather was cool that day and I was feeling better after fifteen days of mourning. The moment I sat on my office chair with a mug of coffee in hand, Romila Kaul, my boss, came to my seat. Her face looked saintly to me for the first time in life. May be I had started to like every face that didn't resemble that of Purnima.

"I want to see the copy of the ad campaign we discussed yesterday," she said without formal greetings.

"Yes ma'am. I will show you in the afternoon," I said matter-of-factly, knowing well that completing the work that soon would be a tough task. It didn't matter because now I was ready for any disaster in life, after the Purnima's case.

The fair-skinned Romila Kaul was a Kashmiri *pundit* settled in Delhi. She was known for her fashion sense. People also appreciated the way she talked, that I found phony. She looked pretty, in spite of the thick-rimmed eyeglasses she wore. She wanted her staff to come in formals while she always wore strange dresses, sometimes resembling those of tribals of the Andaman Islands. I wondered from where she got all those curious clothes. You couldn't find those clothes in shopping markets of my locality Laxmi Nagar, frequented by middle class people. I could bet she must be spending 3 hours everyday getting ready for the office as colors of her clothes and accessories matched every single day I saw her in office. It's nothing less than a feat to maintain this kind of style. I suspected she must be getting half of her salary just for her sense of dressing, as she never looked as busy in work as lesser mortals like us.

Romila used to glow every time someone praised her looks, clothes or just anything remotely related to her. You could see a spark in her eyes on those moments. She loved to be surrounded by sycophants who kept her flattered by their glowing remarks.

I had heard some stories about her past. I was told that in her younger days, she had a boyfriend, who was a struggling actor in Mumbai. She financially supported him and later married him expecting him to make it a name in the film industry. She divorced him when he failed to make his mark, and later married a rich man, who was in his forties.

Kishenjeet Foundation, the organization we all were serving, was into education. It was my first job in the education industry. After working in the IT industry, this organization seemed laidback to me. The unscrupulous promoter Kishenjeet

Singh had devised a way to take money out of the pockets of the innocent boys and girls coming to Delhi in search of good education. The courses on the latest fad MBA were selling like hot cakes. In the name of donation those students had to shell out large amounts of money, hard-earned by their parents living in villages and small towns. Some parents had to sell their lands in rural areas to fund this 'education'. Poorly-paid young chaps masquerading as faculty were doling out 'world-class education' with 'international exposure'. Beautiful girls working as counselors used to attract boys coming from small towns in search of both good education and girlfriends.

I was told that Kishenjeet Foundation was running Kishenjeet University and was doing roaring business before the Supreme Court ordered its closure in February 2005, along with other 116 private universities. Now it was just a shadow of its old form. Now it was running various colleges offering any and every course that market demanded, after getting affiliation from various state universities.

Our marketing and communication department had the thankless job of marketing various courses using the mediums like the Internet, brochures and newspaper ads.

I saw the smiling face of Suraj coming to the office.

"How are you feeling these days," he asked sympathetically.

"I feel better," I said unwillingly.

"One day you will get a nice girlfriend who will take care of you," he tried to make me feel good.

"Thanks for the wishes. But I have had enough of girls now," I said, and added, "I am fine as a single." Deep down in my heart I knew I was not.

Suraj understood my mood and changed the topic. Both of us didn't like our bosses, past or present. We had no other way to feed ourselves, except slaving away under some jerk in a big city away from our parents and families. I was sick of my all bosses. I had seen them all exploiting, manipulating and humiliating their staff. May be all bosses were bad, or maybe I was unlucky. In my life I had seen them having fun by making the staff suffer. Bosses liked only sycophants and it was difficult for me to wag my tail in front of the boss, I felt. Hard work and honesty didn't pay in real life was all I had learnt in my career till that date. I had seen many manipulating guys play their way up to the top, while simpletons like us kept suffering at the bottom. One of my past bosses did not give me a well-deserved promotion claiming that I had an 'attitude problem'. In his eyes, if you didn't lick his ass then you had an attitude problem.

I wanted to start my own company. And I felt Suraj also wanted to do something similar.

"I keep thinking about what to do in my life these days," informed Suraj.

"Ok," I said without showing any interest.

"May be you will also do so once you have enough of love affairs and breakups," he smiled. I smiled back.

"No. I mean I want to start my business. But do not have any idea what exactly I want to do and how. I also don't have enough money," I explained. "Controlling one's natural instincts is next to impossible. I am fighting with my hormones. You know, I find girls with beautiful eyes irresistible," I said.

"We must do something in the IT industry as we have experience in the same," Suraj said.

I nodded.

"Happy birthday," Priya greeted and shook my hands when I reached the office that day. Oh my God, a girl could make you feel so disoriented that you forgot your birthday, I thought, thinking about Purnima. I thanked Priya.

Soon, I was flooded with greetings. I was called into the cabin of Romila. I wondered what she had in her vicious mind. I looked suspiciously at her when I entered the spacious cabin. She surprised me by saying something I wanted to hear, "We want you to be happy." I was touched! How carefully chosen words! Romila could make for a great copy writer, I thought. I thanked her and went back.

I ended the day at the office by cutting the birthday cake. I was also presented a large bouquet. I always thought birthday cake cutting ceremony was a useless Western import to India. On that day suddenly it felt useful. The stupid formalities made me feel good! That night I had a nice sleep after many days. It was wonderful to be appreciated for what you were.

❑

Past Imperfect

I wanted to find out the next big idea to make it big in the world of business. But I was stopped in the mid way by my raging hormones. As a young man you need your quota of romance before settling for a business idea that requires your hard work, time and mind space. My mind was full of thoughts for girls. I used to look at faces of random girls at random places and tried to find resemblance of their face with that of Purnima. It was crazy. I never shared these things with anyone suspecting he would feel I had gone mad.

Breakups have their strange ways. First you feel relieved, then feel sad, then angry, then sad again and finally at peace with yourself, all within a period of four to six months, or more, depending on the length and depth of your relationship. I found it hard to maintain my interest in a girl for more than six months. Mine seemed more like one-sided affairs, unrequited love. The closest I ever reached to a girl was when Purnima called me her 'best friend'. It seemed a big deal on the day. Now I understood this is a useless phrase girls used when they felt like using a boy for emotional support, before dropping him like garbage in a dust bin. I suspected I was the only young boy in the city who had never kissed a girl in entire life. It seemed like one big rejection by the entire community of the fairer sex.

I had one bad experience with a girl in my college days. I was attracted to a traditional girl name Sonia. Small towns of India used to be quite hostile to young lovers. Even if you just talked to a girl on a road, people gave you a stare as if you were having sex with her in full public view. It was jealousy and frustration garbed in the clothes of self-righteousness.

I met Sonia at the British Institute of Spoken English, an institute offering English speaking courses. The Delhi-returned promoter of the institute, Suraj Gupta, exploited middle class people's desire to speak English fluently, and made it a thriving local business. Boys used to join the classes hoping to get a good job in big cities while girls joined hoping for a better groom, or simply out of boredom. I joined the institute to find an audience who could listen to me speaking in English. I was above average in studies - excellent in languages and social studies while pathetic in mathematics and sciences.

Soon after joining, I became a star student of the institute. The promoter used to take me to meet prospective clients on his scooter. In front of parents of young boys and girls he used to make me speak in English to advertise his institute, taking credit for whatever I spoke. The poor parents didn't know that my language was good due to reading English newspapers as I took interest in current affairs. I felt like a public relations tool in the hands of Mr. Gupta. He focused on enrolling young girls, expecting boys to enroll following them. The idea worked big time!

I found Sonia to be a spunky and confident girl with a never-say-die spirit. I soon fell in love with her. Her big eyes took my heart away. My whole body language was shouting that I was in love. When a boy is in love everyone knows. Soon, my classmates came to know about it. Sonia initially took interest in me, even accepting a gift of painting from me. However, she freaked out when she became aware about rumours liking her with me. She started to avoid me fearing disrespect to her family by the society. Mr. Gupta warned me about not chasing Sonia as her father was a police inspector. May be he thought it was a crime to love a girl.

I felt bad when she started ignoring me. I left the institute. I had never met Sonia outside the institute. One day, on her birthday I waited for her outside the institute with a gift for her. After a long wait, I saw her coming out on the road with a girl from the same institute. When I wanted to talk to her, she declined to speak to me saying she would talk to me only inside the institute premises. My heart was broken.

I decided to never follow her. After all I couldn't compromise my self-respect for getting attention of a girl, I thought. I also didn't want to create troubles for her as she belonged to an orthodox family. I didn't have the willingness to go to her father to ask for her hand as I was a student, financially dependent on my father. It was my first heart break, which kept me depressed for the next six months.

Secretly, I felt jealous of Suraj, who had a steady girl friend for last two years. He must have kissed his girl friend, I suspected. I was busy in my romantic day-dreaming when I was called to the Romila's cabin for a team meeting.

Romila had this curious habit of having a meeting of the team in her large cabin regularly. She never informed you about the agenda in advance. I suspected she used to hold meetings just to show to us who was the boss. It was a kind of ego massaging for her.

We all gathered inside her spacious and well-decorated cabin. Her large chair and table made the rest of us look small. Romila's secretary Shaan Bose was a middle-aged short-heighted man, who maintained a low profile. In a way he was opposite of her. He was straight but boring man who was careless about his looks. After we all settled down in the cabin, Romila started to talk with effective dramatic poses, taking care that her lipstick didn't get smeared. She was looking attractive as usual, dressed in white top and grey long skirt. She maintained herself so well that she looked like a 24-year old when she was actually 35 years of age. Some people claimed it was due to her strict dieting.

Romila's petite figure was making her look small compared to her chair and table. As usual Romila asked our opinion about a project. We, around ten of us, started to come up with suggestions and she started to reject them all one by one. At last she gave her views, and we felt under immense pressure to nod our heads like zombies. Mr. Shaan kept taking notes obediently.

"Why she calls a meeting when she already has her opinion formed?" I said angrily to Suraj after the meeting ended.

"This makes her feel good about herself," Suraj chuckled. "All bosses are the same."

"You are right. She has huge ego that regularly needs massaging. Though, have you seen how she behaves with visitors? She acts as if she is the most humble person in the world," I added.

"Many people show false modesty and feel proud about it. She is among them," Suraj supplied.

“Good morning, Amit,” shouted Shantanu Basu when I entered the office the next day.

“Same to you! How was the trip?” I asked.

“Great as usual,” he replied cheerfully. Then we hugged.

Shantanu Basu, my colleague and a friend, had just come back from his home town Kolkata. His looks were nothing to write about. He was short and bespectacled, with receding hairline. I never saw him in casual clothes as he was always dressed in white shirt and black pants with a clean shave. I used to tease him by calling him a ‘pseudo-intellectual’, as he always felt the need to be recognized as an intellectual keeping up with the great intellectual tradition of West Bengal. Though I felt he was more like a mugger who could cram facts but couldn’t come up with original ideas or thoughts. He used to spend half of his office hours searching for Bengalis who had done some notable work or were in notable positions. He never forgot to boast about them to us. Once he was describing achievements of a high-profile Bengali who turned out to be just an executive working for the famous investor George Soros. It was easy to mistake that he was talking about Soros himself.

As an intellectual, Shantanu Basu loved books a lot. He had a good collection of literature that included many classics. He had a hobby of writing poetry. Once he tried to get his collection of poetry published. After five months of sending the collection written in English to all leading publishers, all he got was the note ‘Sorry. We do not publish poetry’. Now he had turned into a respectable blogger, with sizable followers. He was also a mimic, who entertained us sometimes by mimicking our colleagues. Shantanu was too nice to many people. I felt several times people took advantage of his nicety to their advantage.

He was very much scared of dogs. Whenever, he saw a dog he reacted with fear and the dog reacted with suspicion and barking. Thus, the feeling was mutual.

One thing noticeable about Shantanu Basu was his superstitious nature. He had several rings in his fingers all supposed to help him face some problem in life. He had deep faith in astrology, palmistry and numerology. His parents were also into all kinds of mumbo jumbo.

"How are you Mr. Basu?" asked Suraj on seeing Shantanu.

"I am all right. Just had a great trip to my home town," Shantanu replied.

"Let's have a drink today evening! What you say Amit?" Suraj proposed.

"I am ready," I replied.

"What's the plan?" asked Satish, a member of our team.

"A drink party in the evening. You are also invited," said Suraj.

"Sure. You also come, Satish," Shantanu and I said in unison.

Satish was a porn-loving chap of our company. Once Romila caught him watching adult material on his computer, but didn't say anything. The incident didn't change him a bit. He also had a curious habit of sending adult-rated images on email to his friends. Opening his email in the office seemed too much of a risk to me. Shantanu simply used to delete his emails out of fear. Years later I realized staff watching porn in offices is more common than I thought. One of my friends had caught his boss watching porn on his office laptop in the cabin. Another friend, working in a leading ad agency, had the whole team of male members watching porn in office when females were away. Even the manager used to join them. By the way, one day I had caught Romila playing card game on her office desktop.

We met at Suraj's house where he was living alone. After pouring drinks in glasses, Suraj became playful.

"Amit's girl friend has dumped him once again," he said with a wry smile.

"She did not dump me. We ended relationship," I protested.

"Same difference," Satish chuckled picking up his glass.

"Well, he needs sympathy," said Shantanu smilingly. He was a teetotaler. We had cola for him.

"Excuse me. I don't need sympathy. She is already out of my mind," I said trying to look normal while taking a sip from my glass.

"No need to be so much focused on one girl. There are so many around. You can try your luck on any girl of our office," Satish said.

"I don't fancy any of them," I said.

"Because no girl in our office has beautiful eyes. Amit fancies only those girls," supplied Suraj. All three laughed at the suggestion.

"Hi friends, I just forgot to inform you that I am going to get married the next month," informed Shantanu.

"Congrats!" We all said in unison.

"So, where you are having the wedding ceremony and reception?" I asked.

"Marriage in Delhi and reception in Kolkata," Shantanu informed us.

"Great! We'll have some real fun at the event," Suraj said.

Then we toasted to Shantanu's marriage and went for our homes. I and Suraj were living alone in Laxmi Nagar and Noida respectively. Shantanu was with his parents in Noida. Satish was born and brought up in Delhi, and was living with his extended family in Karol Bagh.

After many months I felt footloose and fancy-free, but didn't want to remain so. I set my eyes on a slim Punjabi girl Manjeet Kaur working in our office. She had attractive figure with extra-slim waist. When I used to see her my eyes used to go straight to her waist. One day she caught me staring at her waist when she was coming in my direction. I kept looking at her hourglass figure wrapped in blue jeans and white top, without noticing it was her. I didn't look at her face until she came close to me and said, "good morning." I was embarrassed. She must have felt flattered though!

Oh boy! Girls instinctively know when you feel attracted to them. Soon, I found she was trying to avoid me. In other words, she was playing hard to get.

One fine morning she came to my desk. She looked gorgeous in red *salwar-kameez* with a golden coloured envelop in her hand.

"Hi Amit, good morning! How are you?" She said.

"Same to you! I am fine," I said looking a bit surprised to see her standing close to me.

"My marriage is fixed. Here is the invitation card," she said.

"When..when..?" all I could say.

"The coming Saturday," she said with a smile.

Girls are ruthless, I tell you! I came to know that I was the first person to be invited by her in the entire office. How unkind to do it when she knew that I fancied her!

Of course, I didn't attend her marriage. Most of the office staff members attended her wedding ceremony. The next day, I found many of them talking excitedly about the event, and I felt like slapping many of them.

One evening, I was feeling high after drinking two bottles of beer. Helped by the Dutch courage and pushed by boredom, I called Mansi Singh, a counselor working in the office. She had been working here for long. Till then, I had talked only formally with her. The lanky girl was both ambitious and aggressive, with talent for playing office politics effectively. The dusky damsel was the kind of women who would rise in the corporate world. I proposed to her to watch a film with me. She made some lame excuse for not being able to give me a company.

The next day in the office, I was too embarrassed to look at Mansi. I thought she forgot my proposal. I decided to maintain a low profile for some days. Two days later, she took her revenge in the front of several members of the staff.

"You know what? Amit proposed me to watch a film together two days back," she said and started to laugh loudly.

All eyes were on me. I was embarrassed and speechless. Why the hell she was laughing, I thought. After all she was a girl and it was perfectly ok for a boy to want to watch a film with her! May be she was making fun of my courage to ask her, a senior to me in the organization, for a movie.

"What's wrong about it? You should have gone out together," replied Priya.

Mansi gave Priya a dirty look.

Mansi was insecure about her skin colour, which was dusky. She was a perfect customer, fairness cream makers look for. A heavy amount of fairness cream was pasted on her face all the time. Always dressed in western clothes, she wanted to project herself as a hard-core professional. She seemed to share a weird relationship with Romila. Many times I had seen Mansi standing close to Romila's chair in her cabin with her body touching Romila's body. It was easy to suspect a lesbian relationship between them. After Mansi's refusal to go out with me, my suspicion grew stronger.

Later I came to realize that Mansi was attracted to Bablu Singh, a boast of the highest grade, working in our organization in the marketing department. Bablu was a short-heighted man, always clean-shaven and dressed immaculately. He was a *paan*-chewing spoilt brat of a senior bureaucrat based in Delhi. He never ever lost an opportunity to boast about his father's position, and his almost every sentence started with 'my father….' The way he talked about his father it was natural for anyone to presume that his father was Rajinikanth, the South Indian film star. Needless to say, it was irritating to hear pompous stories of a public servant. After politicians, it was bureaucrats who were making all efforts to ruin this country while making money using corrupt practices, I thought.

One day Bablu was found boasting about how he beat up an old man, an MLA from Uttar Pradesh, after dragging him out of his car. He even slapped his wife when she intervened. It happened when the driver of the MLA car was honking behind Bablu's car. Bablu knew his father would save him from prosecution and he did. I could see an expression of disgust on everyone's faces, when he kept boasting on and on about the incident. Only if Bablu knew his semi-feudal mentality was nothing short of disgusting and distasteful!

The day of Shantanu's marriage come. All team members of the office attended the event held in Noida. Satish and I feasted our eyes on gorgeous Bengali girls before attacking tasty snacks served there. In weddings, there is a sort of competition among girls to look better that others. Shantanu, surprisingly, looked handsome in his golden-coloured *kurta* decorated with embroidery work, and his headgear hiding his receding hairline. He looked very happy to be finally married. I knew he wanted to get married for long, fearing his father might face problems finding bride for his thirty-four year old son.

Shantanu was busy in arrangements but spared time to spend with us. Romila was surprisingly dressed in a green sari, eliciting many compliments from her juniors.

Satish had brought a half bottle of whisky along with him. Satish, Suraj and I took small drinks along with snacks standing in a corner hiding from other team members. We had no space left in the stomach for dinner.

Attending wedding ceremonies have a strange impact on people. Bachelors secretly wish to get married, while already married people feel proud of their marital status. In my case I felt bad that I didn't have a girl in my life. Suraj had a girlfriend, Satish was already married with a son and Shantanu also finally married. Suddenly it seemed bad to be a single. I got determined to learn the art of wooing girls and find a sweet one for me.

The very next day I came to office early and decided to search online about tips to woo girls. Romila's late coming to office seemed like a boon. Orkut was banned in the office after Romila found out that many members of the staff were using the website frequently. Facebook was yet to become fashionable among youth at that time. I searched many dating tips sites. Most of the advices seemed useless. Some tips seemed convincing but didn't work in real life, like trying to keep a girl happy by treating her like a princess! In my case it didn't seem to work at all. My personal experience was that the more I liked a girl and the more I treated her well, the less she was interested in me! Understanding women is almost impossible to men, I tell you!

"What attracts a girl to a boy?" I hit Suraj with this question the moment he came to the office.

"Here you go. Expected of you!" said Suraj with a smile. He knew I was kind of desperate for a girlfriend.

"Don't you want me to be happy in a relationship?" I gave him a dirty look.

Suraj tried to explain, "Well, I think it is difficult to explain. It may be a couple of things. Like confidence of a man. They like a man with confidence to face the problems of the world."

"Good. What more?" I prodded him.

"Sense of humour is also important. You need to keep a girl entertained. They hate bores like you." Suraj gave a big laugh.

"Excuse me, I am not a bore!" I protested.

"But you are slavish to girls. A girl can mould you any way she wants. They like a man with his own personality, tastes and opinions," he said.

"You mean I should not care about their wishes?" I wanted an explanation.

"No. I mean just be yourself," he reasoned.

"What more?" I asked.

"Enough for today! I have some urgent work to do," Suraj said and soon immersed himself in his work.

I continued my search for enlightenment on my office computer.

Soon, I got addicted to learning about how to attract girls. Most advices seemed bullshit but some were good. I engaged Suraj couple of times more in discussions in the hope of finding some gems about how to attract pretty young things.

My research continued for six months occupying most of my mind space. The conclusion was this – women get attracted to men who are confident, have sense of humour, and have their own personality. They also want the men to be unpredictable, as they love surprises. If you have none of the qualities then you better be rich!

One fine day I woke up with a desire to own a bike. It was surprising as I had no interest in automobiles at all. On the other hand, my brothers and cousins were crazy about cars and bikes and could keep taking about them for hours and hours. In fact I felt like slapping anyone who talked about automobiles for long, as I had heard enough of auto talks in the past.

Anyway, the next day in the morning I was at a Bajaj Auto showroom. After all the documentation and signing on many papers, by the evening an executive came close to me.

"Sir, here is the key. You bike is ready. Take it home," He said with a fake smile.

I felt nervous as I didn't know how to ride a bike. If fact I had thought they would take some days in the documentation and on the day of the delivery I would take a friend along who would ride me home. After a lot of thinking with the key in my hand, I approached the executive.

"Hi, there is a problem I don't know how to ride a bike. Can you help me?" I asked feeling embarrassed.

"Sure. I have a guy. Give him 100 bucks. He will drop both of you and the bike to your home," he said after thinking for a while.

Now I owned a bike, but neither knew how to ride it nor had a driving license. For the next four months the bike was parked near my house, while I arranged the license with the help of a broker as I didn't want to deal with corrupt and lazy government employees.

One day I took home Suraj to train me how to ride a bike. He gave me instructions for ten minutes and then went away as he had some urgent work to do. It was not enough.

On a fine morning I sat on the seat of the bike and decided to take it to the office. It was risky as I had not learnt how to ride it properly. I took the gamble anyway. On the 40km long way to my office based at Mohan Cooperative Industrial Estate on Mathura Road, the bike engine got stopped at all red lights as I didn't know how to use gears properly. After some days I got better at riding.

Riding Bajaj Pulsar was cool only if there was no traffic. In the rush hour of traffic it was hardly enjoyable. Riding a bike on Delhi roads made me realize how stupid many drivers are and how they felt more than happy to break traffic rules. Thanks to them, on average five people lose their lives on the Delhi roads every day.

❑

Shruti

That day office seemed buzzing with hectic activities. I came to know that new recruitments were going on. We saw new faces going to the HR department, located in the left corner of the office building. One remarkable thing about the HR department was that it had five staff and four of them were 'managers'. One was Vice President-HR Department, another Senior Manager-HR Department, the third was Manager-HR Department and the fourth was Assistant manager-HR Department. The only non-manager was the newly-joined trainee Kavita Yadav, who was just an 'Executive-HR Department'. So, it took four managers to manage one executive! The promoter Kishenjeet Singh had a policy of doling out high-profile positions without matching compensations.

A piece of news was also waiting for me. Suraj wasted no time in letting me know that there were rumours that Shantanu Basu had married a divorced woman, who was his classmate in his college. We wanted to confirm it with Shantanu himself who was coming the next day to office after his honeymoon.

The very next day, we welcomed back Shantanu to office and wanted to know the authenticity of the rumours.

Predictably, it was embarrassing for him. Sitting beside me in a cushy chair he turned red. We didn't want to spoil his mood as he looked happy after spending time with his wife for a week. However, our curiosity got better of us.

"Hey, you can be frank with us yaar. After all we are friends," said Suraj.

"Well, it's true. Pujita Joseph was my classmate in college. I could not express my love to her. She married a mutual friend, who she loved. Her first marriage didn't work. I proposed to her after her divorce," Shantanu said.

"It's ok. How are things now?" I asked.

"I am very happy," Shantanu said beamingly.

"I had to change my religion for marriage. I am now a Christian," he informed us.

"What?" I was surprised. Changing religion for a bloody marriage! I knew Shantanu's parents must have been hurt due to his conversion. Suddenly I noticed Bablu coming close to us.

"What? You're a Christian now? My father knows many Christians. In his service, he works with people of all religions. By the way, the last week he went to Kashmir on an official trip. He was given a salute of 20 tanks. He was so respected there you know." Bablu want into a monologue.

Who the fuck cared about his damn dad! Only after leaving the job I came to know that most of his boastings were pure lies, intended to impress people and boost his position in the organization. And his father was not actually working at the senior position he claimed.

"So, that girl made you change your religion? Was it a condition for marriage?" Suraj asked Shantanu, ignoring Bablu.

"Yes," said Shantanu looking dejected.

"Oh fuck!" came out of Suraj's mouth.

"There was another reason why I married her. An astrologer told me that marrying a divorcee will ensure a great financial and personal success for me in life, when I consulted him before the marriage. He also told me that I could still remain a Hindu in spite of converting to Christianity," said Shantanu.

"How come?" Suraj asked.

"He organized a *pooja* and *havan* at my home for that," Shantanu said. Bablu silently went away as no one was listening about his father's exploits.

"It's not possible to belong to two religions. How much he charged?" Suraj asked.

"Forty thousand rupees," Shantanu said.

"Idiot, he fooled you!" I told Shantanu.

I felt bad for Shantanu. I knew he belonged to a conservative family. It must be painful for his parents considering he was the lone child of them. Later I came to know that his wife Pujita had put some other conditions too. One condition was that Shantanu's parents had to not live with him. Now he was living with his wife in Noida, while his parents lived alone in Kolkata at their ancestral house. It didn't seem fair.

Coming to the office on time was a challenge that I had to face every day. Four hours of daily commuting was tiring.

That day, the moment I came inside the office, I spotted a beautiful girl. Dressed in red top and black jeans she looked stunning. I noticed her smouldering eyes and full lips. Our eyes met. My heart skipped a beat. Time stood still for few moments. Something magical happened inside me. I could not take my eyes off her. She walked past me while I tried to control myself.

I came to sit on my chair still thinking about her. Satish came to my seat to inform me about a new attractive girl who had joined the organization. By his description I knew it was she. He told me her name was Shruti. Soon I realized she had created a minor flutter in the office. Leaving my past behind, I decided to try my luck on her. At the worst I would end up being what I was - a single.

Shruti was sitting beside Mahesh, a senior counselor. He was also a faculty of hospitality courses. With his young age of twenty-five and his humble manners, he was popular among students. He used to call students 'bacche' though he looked like a 'baccha' himself. I approached Mahesh and greeted him hoping to get introduced to Shruti. Thankfully it worked.

"Hi, I am Amit, the copy writer," I said, while shaking hand of Shruti sitting on a chair beside Mahesh.

"I am Shruti, a new counselor," she introduced herself. She was well-prepared for the first day in the office. I noticed her make-up closely. The lip gloss was making her lips look full and shining. The use of shadow on eyes made them look highly attractive. The light perfume smell was slowly driving me crazy. For such a pretty girl, she was given the thankless job of brainwashing young students into getting admission in various courses, using her charm and promising 'international-level' careers.

I noticed she had opened a web page on astrology on her computer. I was in a flirting mood.

"Astrology? Oh yes, you must be nervous on the first day

on the job. But don't worry! As far as you keep me happy your job will be perfectly safe here," I said tongue firmly in the cheek.

She gave me a dirty look. I smiled. Looking into her eyes, I felt like kissing her. After some random chatting, I soon went back to my desk keeping the first meeting short and sweet.

For the next ten working days, I kept going to Shruti's desk in the evening after getting some time. I, Shruti and Mahesh used to chat about several topics, including personal life, hobbies, funny incidents and films. Shruti was opening up with me, sharing with me her personal life. She belonged to Patna, living in Delhi with her brother. She had spent many years of her life in Gujarat and got higher study from there. Her father was a doctor, and mother a lecturer in Magadh University in Bihar.

I didn't visit her desk for the next two days, to create curiosity in her mind and to see her reaction. On third day, in the evening she was standing by my desk smiling. She was dressed in a grey top and blue jeans. Her eyes were sparkling in spite of day-long work that had left her looking a bit tired. Most of the staff had left for home by then.

"Hey, what happened? You didn't show your face for two days?" She was curious to know. She looked surprised why I didn't visit her workstation for last some days. Girls like surprises and unpredictability, I tell you!

"Nothing, just more work," I replied smilingly.

She pulled a chair and sat beside me and started to chat. She was sitting so close to me I was feeling hot. May be it was due to the high temperature in her body. I began to sweat. She was curious to know what I was doing.

"So, what do you do here?" She asked.

"Nothing. Just wasting time on Orkut all the day," I said deadpan. She smiled.

"What did you do in last two days?" She asked.

"Just thinking about you all the day," I said.

"Stop flirting with me," she said. I could guess she also liked flirting like all other girls in the world.

It seemed she was into me already. Soon, she started to call me at lunch time and I started to have lunch with her. Suraj and Shantanu knew why I was not having lunch with them.

Shruti was like an oasis in the desert of office. Later I was informed that some young guys of the office proposed to Shruti and got rejected. It felt good to be with a girl in demand.

One day Suraj asked me, "So, how are things going on with Shruti?"

"Nothing much. She is a sweet girl," I said.

"I know. I noticed she has beautiful eyes, your weakness," Suraj laughed. I laughed back.

Shruti's presence in my life changed me. I started coming to the office early in the morning, so that I could have more time to chat with her near the coffee dispensing machine. I started to take more care of myself. Sometimes I found myself smiling, thinking about Shruti. I got some pairs of clothes on weekend – new jeans and T-shirts. There was no official rule to wear only formals in the office. I loved informal clothes as they made me feel relaxed. Another big change was that I hit the gym to take better care of my body. Going to gym makes you feel good, I tell you. It gives you confidence too.

"I can see your biceps. Have you hit the gym?" asked Suraj one day.

"Yes," I smiled.

"Good going," Suraj said rolling his eyes.

Now I was spending days talking to Shruti, and nights wondering how to take things forward in the relationship. I decided to take some initiatives. It was risky as a rejection would break my heart and discourage me from making further moves.

"Want to see the film *Krrish*? It has got good reviews in the papers." I proposed to her at her desk one evening.

"Sorry, I have already seen the film with my brother," she replied firmly with a smile.

"Ok. Then let's watch *Fanaa*? It's also good, I have heard," I said, giving her an alternative.

"Oh, I have seen too," she said, sounding rather unconvincing.

I was disappointed. I wondered if she was telling me the truth. I thought maybe I was making moves too fast.

I wanted to say a lot of nice things to her. Praise her beauty or write a poem about the beauty of her eyes. However, I resisted my temptation. After all these things didn't work with

Purnima. I couldn't believe I had written a long nice poem praising Purnima's eyes. I remembered she had liked it, but it didn't help our relationship. The poem was still with me in my email account. Someday I could recite the same to Shruti, I thought, but not before she became my true girlfriend. No girl became your true girlfriend unless you had kissed her on the lips, I thought.

Shantanu seemed to be going through some troubles those days. We thought he was missing his parents. We knew he adored them, but was forced to live without them due to his wife. His father, Debojit Basu, was a true gentleman. I was told he had a thriving bakery business in West Bengal before suffering a major loss in the venture, after getting deceived by a cousin. Now he was living a retired life. He had accepted his son's decision to live alone with wife, wishing a good married life for him.

Shantanu used to come to the office late at 11 am and leave early. We were expecting him to soon get a piece of advice from the boss.

"What's the matter dear? You look disturbed these days." Suraj asked him one day.

"No. Nothing," Shantanu replied trying hard to look normal.

"Hey, don't try to fool us. There must be some issue in your personal life," I insisted.

"Just some minor issues at home. I am worried about my parents living in Kolkata," Shantanu revealed.

"Why don't you simply take them here?" Suraj was curious to know.

"No, Pujita doesn't want that," he said.

"You are such a hen-pecked husband. I would never do that," Suraj said.

"We'll see once you get married," Shantanu said.

"By the way Suraj, do you have any plans for marriage with Ritu?" I asked Suraj.

"Well, I have not discussed this topic with my parents yet. They are quite conservative. I'll talk about it at the right time," Suraj said.

"Conservative? It won't be easy then," I said.

"Doesn't she want to marry you? Doesn't she want you to talk to your parents?" Shantanu asked.

"Yes, she does," Suraj said.

We all had interesting cases. One was married but not happy, another had girlfriend but no plans of marriage, and here I was pursuing a girl. Well, in case of Satish, there was a happily married man addicted to porn.

In the morning the first thing I do in the office is to get a mug of coffee and then check emails. The latest email that attracted me was from Satish containing adult content. I got tempted to open the email. The moment that email opened a topless model was displaying her assets. Before I could feast my eyes on the gorgeous model, I heard a sweet female voice. Instantly, I closed the webpage and looked up.

"Hi, good morning," Shruti said standing close to me. She was looking fresh and cheerful in a yellow top and a white long skirt.

"Same to you," I replied and pulled a chair for her. I had this curious habit of replying with the phrase 'same to you' in response to formal greetings. Once I ended up saying 'same to you' when someone had wished me good luck on my impending journey.

"What you are doing this weekend," Shruti asked sitting on the chair. I wondered why she was asking that.

"Nothing much. Just relaxing and watching TV," I replied.

"Let's watch *Fanaa* at Priya cineplex," she proposed.

I was surprised. She rejected my proposal when I offered her and now she was proposing herself. It is indeed difficult to understand the women psychology! I wanted to say yes before she changed her mind. However, I decided to play harder to get.

"But I thought you have already watched it?" I asked her sarcastically.

"Yes, but I want to watch it again. So, are you coming?" She asked.

"Well, I will find time for that," I said trying to hide my happiness at her proposal.

"Is evening show ok with you?" She asked, as if she had all planned in advance.

"Yes," I said. She didn't know that any show with her was ok for me.

"Ok. See you on the weekend," she said and went away. The past disappointment had gone away and I was feeling elated.

That evening was the best I ever had in my life till that day. Before the show, we had Pepsi and burgers at McDonald's.

Thankfully, it was not crowded. It was so nice to see her outside the office. We talked freely about lots of things.

"I have heard you sing well," she asked. I didn't know who had told her so. Maybe she was simply teasing me. I decided to play along.

"People say so," I replied.

"Can you sing couple of lines now?" She requested.

"But there is one requirement to be fulfilled before I sing a song," I said.

"What is that?" She asked.

"I sing songs only when there is a beautiful girl in front of me," I said hiding my laughter.

"You mean I am not beautiful?" She asked punching my left arm.

The film had already started when we entered the cinema hall. We had corner seats. Though it was of no use as it was beginning of our friendship and I had no guts to do any romantic activity in the darkness of the hall. Our hands touched once in the darkness, but I didn't try to hold her hands as I thought she was not yet ready for that.

The film was over at 8pm. Performances were ok but the movie was not great, and I could find out some loopholes in the script. Shruti liked the film and she was not concerned at all about technicalities like script. I think most of the audiences are like her only, who only care about how they feel inside the hall. No wonder filmmakers release many movies even without a story or a script.

"My birthday is coming. What will you gift me?" Shruti asked me when we were preparing to go home.

"Well, I gift only kisses to girls on their birthdays!" I said half-jokingly.

She gave me a dirty look.

"You can tell me the budget and I will shop any item of my choice as a birthday gift from you," she said pointing a finger towards items being sold at the shopping complex.

"I told you what I gift to girls. If you want I can give you that right now," I teased her. She pinched my arm to show her disapproval.

I decided to give her a ride on my bike to her home. While pillion riding, she made sure her body didn't touch mine. It was a pleasant evening of spring. I could feel romance in the air.

"You know Amit, many people told me that Delhi is unsafe for girls. But I never felt that way here," she said while enjoying the ride.

"You will never get eve-teased if you take lift from eve-teasers," I said. She gave a laugh.

When we reached near her house, before biding me bye, she complained, "You didn't give me birthday gift."

"As I told you I can give you right now. Come close to me," I said removing my helmet and trying to bring some romance in my voice.

"No. I don't need that," she said looking confused and shy. I smiled.

While returning my home, I repented not kissing her in the cinema hall. But one bad move and your relationship goes off-track. I didn't want to make some big mistake at that point of time. Any rejection by a girl feels like hell, I tell you!

I kept reliving the meeting with her in my mind throughout the night. I decided I would try to kiss her on the next date.

The next day in the office suddenly it was feeling hot in the day time. Soon, we realized the air-conditioner of the office was not working. The centralized air-conditioner had some technical fault. We were forced to work in the hot and humid atmosphere. We were informed about the technical fault.

The next day I lost my patience and went to the administration head to complain. I returned without complaining when I saw him sweating like a pig in his cabin in vest, while using a newspaper as a hand fan.

Romila decided to have one regular team meeting in a nearby restaurant Ruby Tuesday. A large separate table was booked for us in advance by Romila's secretary Shaan. We were around twelve people. We all were happy at the prospect of free snacks and beer. This idea worked for us. The male members of the team were serviced beer in the beginning of the meeting. It later helped us suffer boring and ego-boosting lectures of Romila easily. The girls preferred fruit juice. As usual Bablu started one of his 'my papa' stories. He also knew how to massage Romila's ego by flattering her in team meetings!

Just before the meeting formally began Romila's mobile rang. She picked up the phone. Everyone was silent to let the boss complete the call. Romila sounded a bit angry with an executive of her bank on the phone. She began to shout on the phone while we were stunned.

A couple of minutes later she put her phone down and said, "These motherfu***** are chu***."

We were shocked! There was a pin-drop silence for a minute! We couldn't digest the fact that this supposedly sophisticated lady could use choicest of earthy expletives.

Romila smiled, composed herself and went inside her fake skin. The meeting started with her giving her usual lecture, the same given in every meeting.

I was enjoying free beer too much to focus on what Romila was saying. All I could gather that Romila had made Mansi our team leader. What the fuck! She had no sense of copy or design, and counseling doesn't make you eligible for handling creative people, I thought! Soon, we noticed that the early low-volume soft music in the restaurant was growing louder.

Romila wanted to talk to the restaurant's manager. Suraj called the manager.

"Excuse me, we are having a very important official meeting here. Can you turn down the music volume please?" She asked the manager.

"Sorry ma'am, our regular customers want loud music," he answered politely.

Romila continued her lecture to the team. She was getting increasingly distracted by the laud music. Some of us were enjoying both beer and music, much to the chagrin of Romila.

After some time, Romila again requested the manager to turn down the music volume without success. Now it was playing the hit number *'Bheegey Honth Tere Pyaasa Dil Mera'* from the Hindi film *Murder*. Finally, Romila was delivering the pep-talk almost shouting while the high volume peppy music was making us tap our feet under the table. It was a weird fusion of office keywords like 'quality', 'hard work', and 'target' with the song words like 'dil,' 'pyaasa' and 'tan'. The most interesting office meeting I ever had! We kept laughing about it for a long time.

Later Romila realized her mistake and never held any meeting in a restaurant.

We were finalizing the ad copy and design to be published in the Times of India. I had finally checked and approved it. At the last moment the promoter Kishenjeet Singh came, suggested many changes and gave approval to the changed copy and design on the spot.

In a tearing hurry the ad copy was sent to the newspaper and the very next day it was there in a full page advertisement. Then we noticed a glaring grammatical mistake in the copy, all approved by the promoter himself. Lacking guts to pinpoint Mr. Singh for the error, Romila gave me an earful blaming me for the mistake. If you poke your fucking nose in my work then don't blame me for the errors, I felt like telling Romila.

One evening, I was going to the loo, when I saw Romila coming towards me.

"I want to discuss the article you are writing for the website," she said.

"Excuse me ma'am, I am just coming back from the restroom within two minutes," I said politely.

While returning from the rest room, I met Shruti and went to her desk, forgetting that Romila was waiting for me. I started to chat and laugh with Shruti for half an hour. She gave me her punching card. The card recorded employee arriving and going time. She requested me to punch her card after the office hours. She had to leave office early and didn't want her early leaving marked in the office records. Then she bid me goodbye.

Then I suddenly got reminded of Romila.

I came back to my desk in a hurry to see Romila waiting for me. I profusely apologized for making her wait for me. By looking at her face I knew she had not forgiven me. Suddenly she opened the article I was still writing on my computer, and started to tear it apart. I requested her not to judge or pass comments on the article as I was still in the process of writing it. However, Romila was determined to get the anger out of her system anyway.

I got reminded of punching Shruti card late. After punching at the main exit, I came back to her seat to hide it below her desktop, as requested by her. I had a look at the card. It carried a beautiful smiling passport size photo of her. I looked in all directions. There was no one in sight in the office. I kissed her photo and then slowly put it below her desktop.

The next day, she came to me in tears at lunch time.

"Hey Shruti, what has happened?" I asked her.

She said nothing and signaled me to come to the canteen with her.

"Now tell me what has happened?" I asked her after we had our plates full of dishes.

She started crying. I was shocked. I looked around. The canteen was almost vacant as most of the members of the staff had already taken lunch.

"Hey stop crying. Just relax and then let me know what has happened," I said holding her hand.

She took some time to compose herself.

"My team leader Ahmed publicly humiliated me," she said, still in tears.

"He accused me of not working hard in the team meeting. The reality is that I have given him the most numbers of students, and still he is venting out his frustration on me," she said.

"Any reason for this behavior? Why he is being unfair to you?" I asked her.

"Maybe because I had refused his advances," she said now smiling.

"What?" I was shocked. I left her hand and tried to compose myself.

"Yes, he wanted to watch a film with me when I was new to the company. He tried twice and I rejected both the times. He also doesn't like ours taking lunch together," she said.

"Fuck him!" I said with reasonable anger.

"Yes, he is a big time asshole," she said. I was shocked to hear the cussword from her mouth, a girl's mouth. She understood my feeling.

"When I really hate someone I call the person an asshole," she explained calmly with a smile. I felt better that at least she was smiling.

"Anyway, if he does the same thing ever, you let me know. I will talk to him directly about it," I tried to assure her.

"Don't worry. If he ever does so again, I will go to his boss and make his life miserable," she said with a menacing smile.

"Anyway this is nothing compared to what I had seen in one company," she said with a sad tone.

"What had happened in that company?" I asked.

"In my last job one dirty old man once took hold of my hand when I was alone in the office and said he wanted to come close to me. I got away from him and complained to the boss. Instead of doing something about it, he asked me to resign as the old man was a senior manager in the company," she said deadpan.

"Why didn't you chop the head off the old bastard," I said angrily.

"I didn't want to create a scene for my family. I simply changed the job," she said.

"It's fault of the Indian women that they bear bad behavior from men. This encourages men to keep behaving that way. Men treat women pathetically here, I tell you. I could have killed many men had I been a woman. This is why the Indian woman I admire the most is Phoolan Devi, the Bandit Queen. She really knew how to give a tit for a tat," I said.

"Don't get hyper, my dear friend. Just relax," she said mocking me.

"This is not a joke. I feel strongly about it. The problem is with the society. People condition girls to feel inferior. Boys are made to feel superior to girls in the family. The result is that when boys grow up they feel it's fair to treat women badly. Even the great singer Lata Mangeshkar once said she wanted to be born as a boy in her next life. You can guess what kind of situations women are forced to live in. It's ironic to claim women to be *devis* and then feel ok to treat them badly," I said.

"Oh my God! You can so go on and on about it. Let's end this discussion for the time being," she said raising her hands.

Something was not nice in Suraj's life. I could guess he looked tense for last some days. One day he opened his mouth.

"My parents are not accepting Renu," he said looking down.

"Why? Is it the caste difference?" I asked him while taking a sip from my cup of coffee.

"Yes," he said.

"Damn the caste system! The old crap from the past!" I said.

"Do you believe in the caste system?" Shantanu asked Suraj.

"Of course not. But my parents are hell bent on marrying me to a girl of my caste. I am being shown photos of many girls these days," Suraj said. "I tried to convince them. It didn't work," he added.

"I guess you need to give more time to your parents. They may mellow down," I said sympathetically.

"Will see what happens. Renu is very upset at this. She will not marry any other boy, she says," informed Suraj.

"Relax. Things will get better. Let's have a drink today in the evening. You will feel better," I proposed.

"Yes, that's better," Shantanu supported.

That evening we had drink at my flat. Living alone in a flat was boring and I was happy to play host to friends. I had purposefully maintained a distance from neighbors as I wanted to maintain my privacy. In my last rented stay at Palam Colony in West Delhi I was so friendly with neighbors that I had no privacy. I had a steady stream of visitors, young and old, in my room wanted to have small chats with me. I was as nice as they helped me never feel the need for my family. On the other side, they made it difficult for me to do any important work on my computer at home.

Suraj felt better after few pegs. Shantanu was happy giving us company with a cold drink. I kept thinking about Shruti after two pegs.

It was a memorable day. It was raining heavily since the night and there were heavy traffic jams in the morning. I took great pains to reach office. Many members of the staff came quite late due to rain and traffic jams, while some didn't come. Around 11am, I saw Shruti coming to office, all drenched in rain. Oh god! she was looking stunning in her wet clothes - a white top and blue jeans. Her untied hair was adding to her appearance. Her wet clothes were making her shiver slightly. She greeted me. Soon, she sat with a mug of coffee in her hands with me in the office canteen.

"I didn't want to come to office today due to rains," she said while taking a sip from the cup.

"Thank God, you came," I said.

"What's so good about it?"She asked.

"Your wet clothes are making me turn on," I said, with a mischievous smile.

"Shut up," she said while pinching my hand. I noticed that she was wearing a ring with a strange looking stone in her index finger.

"What's this ring?" I asked her.

"Nothing. It's a long story," she said trying to avoid talking about the ring.

"No problem. Go on with the long story behind that. We have enough time today." I told.

"Well, a *baba* had given me this ring. A couple of years back I was feeling sad and facing some problem. I contacted a *baba* living in Mehrauli in Delhi. He took Rs. 10,000 as change and made me go though many rituals spanning over a month. Later I stopped going to him."

"Why stopped going to him?"

"I stopped because one day he asked me to read an ancient book without clothes," she said with hesitation.

"Oh my God! Are you stupid? How can you go to the frauds, who usually make their living out of fooling illiterate people?" I was shocked.

"It was my error of judgment. I never made any mistake like that," she said with a hollow pride.

That day there was no work in the office as there was no electricity and moreover central air-conditioning was also not working due to water-logging. Shruti went back to her home when she realized no work was possible. The members of our team spent the day just chatting and gossiping. We braved traffic jams and water-logging to go back to our homes.

Soon, I found another opportunity to go out with Shruti. She wanted to shop at Connaught Place, and wanted me to give her company on Friday. We took leave from the office early on that day.

After she had her full quota of shopping, we went to the Central Park. Sitting on a bench and sipping cola, I felt it was the right time to do something important. I was feeling both excited and nervous. I thought trying to kiss her would be better than simply expressing my love for her. She sat close to me.

Her right hand touched my left hand. I took it as a sign that she was ready for the next move.

I took note of her lip gloss, her deep grey eyes and shining cheeks. She was wearing deep green *salwar-kameez* with matching ear-tops.

I imagined kissing her while she kept talking about her first job experience in Delhi. May be she didn't have any idea about what was going in my head, or maybe she knew it and was trying to look ignorant. I came closer to her and tried to take my head close to her. She got a hint of my intentions. She suddenly stopped talking and became still.

"I am engaged," she disclosed with a hesitation.

I was stunned! It was a bolt out of the blue! I was dumbfounded!

I pulled myself behind.

"I am already engaged to Shiv," she continued.

"When...when?" I gathered enough courage to ask.

"The engagement ceremony took place a year back. I had met Shiv Mishra in my high school days. He works in Bangalore," she said with a tinge of sadness.

"So, when are you planning to marry?" I asked after an awkward silence.

"May be the next year," she replied.

There was no need to talk anymore. My dreams had broken once again. I felt shattered inside. I didn't know what more to talk about. The meeting ended abruptly.

I dropped her near her home. We didn't talk much on the way.

I didn't get sleep that night. I kept thinking about Shruti. She should have told me about her relationship status earlier, I felt. I blamed my bad luck for my regular heart-breaks. Why all the boys in the world seemed to have girlfriends, while I was always disappointed? Why it's always me who got his heart broken? I kept thinking without finding any answer.

I and Shruti didn't talk for the next some days. I took lunch with my office pals after many days. They were surprised to see me with them at lunch time. I was sad and heart-broken, and tried to avoid Shruti.

"What's the matter? All ok?" asked Suraj at the lunch table.

"Shruti is engaged," I whispered to him. I found the food of the office canteen tasteless after many days.

"Oh! shit," he said, and reasoned "she should have told you long back, at least couple of months back." I was silent. I was feeling down, and was not interested in either reasoning or calculations. Suraj changed the topic.

"Do you know, Bablu is actually married, and is father of a kid?" He informed me, and added, "he claims to be a bachelor because he wants to flirt with Mansi."

He was expecting me to ask how he knew about that. I was not interested and my face was expressionless.

After a week, I felt guilty because I was not talking to Shruti only because she was engaged to some other guy. I was also missing her. So, one evening I dialed her phone extension in office.

"Hello, Shruti?" I asked on the phone.

"Yes," she said without any emotion.

"What are you doing?" I asked.

"Nothing," she replied.

"Come over here." I invited.

She came over to my desk. She was looking down and tired. I teased her and talked about light things just to cheer her up and to let her know that I was not upset with her after our last meeting. She got the cue and started to talk in her usual way.

The next morning she was waiting at my desk when I came to the office. There was a handsome boy sitting next to her. He looked like a gentleman with his childlike face. He was clean-shaven, and dressed in a blue shirt and black pant. She lost no time in introducing me to the boy.

"Good morning Amit! Meet Shiv my fiancé," she said, still looking tired.

"Hi," I said and shook hand of the boy out of courtesy. Though I didn't feel like even looking at his face.

"I didn't tell you earlier. I am leaving Delhi to go to Bangalore. Shiv is based in Bangalore and he wants me to be there," informed Shruti sounding a bit sad.

"Ok," all I could say. "So, when are you leaving office?" I gathered courage to ask her.

"Today, within an hour. I had already resigned yesterday and the HR department is completing some formalities now," she said.

"Will you come back to Delhi?" I asked.

"No. We plan to settle down in Bangalore," she said slowly.

"I am going to collect my papers from the HR department. Then I will go. It was nice knowing you. Take care of yourself. Good bye," she shook my hand and went away. Shiv also went away after her while waving to me.

I slowly sat down on my chair. I was dumbfounded. I felt as if I was suddenly hit by nervous breakdown. My head went blank.

The day was spent lying low and the night was spent drinking heavily. I emptied a full bottle of whisky in the night. The loneliness of my bedroom was biting me. I was not ready for another heart-break that soon.

Suddenly I heard a very loud sound of loudspeaker from a 'jagran' going on the locality. It was already mid-night and they were disturbing sleep of the neighborhood. The loudspeaker was blaring out a religious song set to the tune of a hit filmi vulgar song. I don't know what kind of religious service is done by disturbing sleep of innocent and peaceful people. Those fools never thought of old people, small babies, students preparing for exams and hard-working office-goers trying to catch their well-deserved sleep, or even a court order to ban use of loudspeakers in the night. Sadistic jobless assholes! We spread too much of filth and pollution in the name of religious activities. I wanted to go out and break the whisky bottles on their heads. I kept on drinking till I fell unconscious on the bed.

The entire office came to know about what happened between me and Shruti. Suraj, Shantanu and Satish came to my desk and said something nice in sympathy. I could not remember what exactly they said due to hangover. I needed some time to get over what had happened. I was cursing my bad luck. Soon,

I also started to miss her like hell. She came into my life like a cool breeze and then suddenly left me behind to feel the heat once again.

I started to drink heavily, and also started to smoke for the first time in my life. Smoking helped in fighting sadness and anxiety in the day time while alcohol helped me sleep in the night. Maybe living in a big city alone without my family I needed an emotional support. Soon, I realized I was suffering from depression. One day out of desperation, I went to a chemist to get some anti-depressants. He refused to give me that without a doctor's prescription.

I didn't call or email Shruti thinking she belonged to some other guy. I was hurt by her sudden departure from my life. She didn't call me. Maybe she felt guilty for breaking my heart. Maybe she didn't want to complicate her life.

Coming to the office every day reminded me of Shruti. I thought perhaps changing the job will help me get over Shruti easily. I started to consider that option. Soon I was sending my resume to several firms.

All was not well in the lives of others too.

"I want to let you know something," Shantanu told Suraj and me one day.

"Sure. Let us know," Suraj said.

"I have filed for divorce," Shantanu said.

"What!" I exclaimed.

"It can't happen so soon," Suraj said, as if it was in his hands.

"Yes. It's true. Pujita wanted so. In couple of months I will be free from her," Shantanu said.

I always knew Pujita was not very happy with Shantanu. Before the marriage she had told him to start smoking and drinking because, hold your breath, it would make him a real man! She found him lacking in manliness. Insulting indeed!

"The way she was putting conditions on you it was bound not to work," Suraj said frankly.

I didn't know how to comfort Shantanu. I didn't feel like doing that either.

"Why didn't you tell us earlier? The process must have taken long time," I asked.

"Well, I was embarrassed to talk about it. My parents have lot of social respect in their society. It was painful for them too," he said with a tinge of disappointment.

"What about the astrologer's prediction of a happy and successful life after marriage with her?" I asked Shantanu.

"I can't reach him. His mobile phone is switched off. He is no longer staying at his old place," Shantanu said.

"It was bound to happen," I said sarcastically.

On Monday, I was feeling a bit uncomfortable in the office without any obvious reason. In the afternoon, Romila called me into her cabin. I nervously went inside. I noticed that in her cabin Mansi and Bablu were also sitting.

"Have a seat Amit. How are you?" Romila said. Her extra-sweet voice made me suspicious of some evil thought going in her head.

"I am fine," I said without any expression on my face.

"Amit, I am not happy with your performance. Even Bablu and Mansi are not happy with your work. Some days back Bablu said you were not working as hard as you could. Mansi says you don't take interest in work. You have to leave this job. Send me your resignation letter. The coming Friday will be your last day at the office," Romila said calmly.

I was shocked to the core. It was completely unexpected. Frankly speaking I never let my personal issues affect my work performance, and even Romila used to like my work just couple of months back. And who is this fucking Bablu to decide about my performance! The stupid boss was really blown away by this asshole's boastings to give him too much importance. Just imagine a marketing guy evaluating work of a creative person! Mansi understood designing and copywriting as much as I understood rocket science. First Romila made this counselor our team leader, and then let this pea-brained girl start giving her opinions about my creative work.

"Have you finished?" I asked Romila.

"Yes," she said.

"Ok. Then let me put my points. And please don't disturb me while I am expressing my views," I said gathering my strength. Romila looked determined to fire me without hearing me out. So, I decided to just say what I felt about her.

"First of all, I am not bothered that you are firing me. Second thing is that you have actually insulted me by making Mansi my team leader as she has neither qualification nor experience to judge my work. The third thing is that is Bablu is not my boss to pass judgment about my work. The fourth thing is, I am sorry to say so, that you encourage politics in the office. Sycophants are promoted while hard-working members of the staff are ignored. The last thing is that if Mansi or Bablu ever felt this way about my work then they should have told me in the past. Firing an employee without a warning or hearing him out is grossly unfair," I concluded.

“I do indeed encourage politics in the office. So what?” Romila said confidently. Her answer was surprising. At least she should have been apologetic about that, I thought. Maybe she thought abusing her power was her birth right. A typical old Indian mentality!

“Guys. Reply to him. You told me you had warned him about his work. Reply to his question,” Romila said while looking at Mansi and Bablu. Both were silent, with heads hanging in embarrassment. They didn’t say anything.

“Ok Amit. You can go now,” Romila said looking a bit embarrassed at silence of her two dear employees.

“Ok, you will get my resignation letter tomorrow,” I said. I had a look at the faces of Mansi and Bablu. Their heads were still hanging in shame.

I felt very bad about getting fired. What I felt even worse was that my sincerity at work was doubted, and people without required qualifications passed biased judgments against me. In the evening, after reaching my home, I felt bad that out of so many staff only I was chosen to be treated unfairly. I drank a lot to forget the humiliating experience. Then I tried to console myself thinking that in our country so many people are treated unfairly. Anyone with any amount of power tends to abuse it, I felt. I became determined that one day I would become far more successful than the stupid Romila.

By the next day, the news had spread in the office about my firing. I didn’t like sympathy in the eyes of the people. Satish hacked office emails of Bablu and Mansi to come up with a proof that they indeed planned my ouster from the organization. He showed me the email exchanges between them as a written proof that they wanted me to go. They had sent some negative feedback about me to Romila using general and subjective terms like 'do not like his work' and 'not working hard' without being specific about a particular work. Using this biased personal opinion anyone could be fired in any company!

The same day evening I submitted my resignation letter to Romila. I stopped going to the office and started looking for a new job sitting at my home. Within a week I got a job in a Noida based company Softdata, operating in knowledge process outsourcing (KPO) sector. It was a BPO company involved in non-voice based outsourcing work.

❑

Softdata

On the very first day I realized Softdata had a different culture compared to my previous job. The company's large building was impressive. The blue-coloured structure was made with generous use of glass. I had in past worked for a smaller IT company offering services to US clients.

The receptionist sitting at large desk greeted me with a formal smile. She thought I was a visitor as she never greeted me even once after she became aware I was a new joinee.

Five other people joined the company with me on that day. We were made to sit in a training room. One new joinee was Supriya Sharma, a talkative and pretty girl. I could bear with her silly talks just due to her beauty. I was trying to avoid looking at her, determined to avoid girls after my past bitter experiences.

After some time a trainer came and introduced himself. We were going to be trained for the next two weeks about the work process. He told us that we had to edit and summarize large amount of content for a US client.

I was impressed to know that the company had more than three thousand staff sitting in the building. The company had four canteens offering more than enough opportunity to waste time, provided you got any spare time. I didn't know why the companies with most taxing work targets had the most amenities for the staff, fully aware that they would get no time to avail of them.

One big attraction of the company was that it had attractive incentives for good performers. Our team had around hundred people, roughly half of them of the fairer sex. For some star performers, the incentives were more than the salary. After finishing the training, we were put on live project work.

I soon realized they were paying nicely for a not-so-nice work. The work was monotonous and mind-numbing. You had to meet the monthly target of work or get a peace of mind from the boss. The monthly targets were based on experience of work in the company.

Sensing a nice amount of money awaiting me at month-end, I worked hard, ignoring everything else.

I earned handsome amount of incentives for the initial some months. With practice, I got better at achieving monthly targets with ease. Soon I was spending half of the office time on work and the rest in lazing away in canteens of the company. When I got tired of spending spare time in canteens, I started to go outside the office and just walking around in nearby Sector 18 market in my spare time.

I was happy at the new office. My colleague Supriya Sharma tried to become friendly with me but I had decided to avoid her after I came to know that she had a boyfriend. I was determined to have nothing to do with girls with a boyfriend or a fiancé. Moreover, I didn't want to get attracted to any girl and miss my monthly work targets.

I kept in touch with Suraj and Shantanu meeting them after regular intervals.

Soon our department saw a new change. A poker-faced bespectacled young man Saurabh Dixit joined our team as the new boss. His first decision was to significantly reduce the amount of incentives offered to employees. It made the top management happy while causing heart-burn among our team members.

Now we were making far less amount of money due to the newly-structured incentive scheme. It seemed useless to work our asses off trying to earn peanuts as incentives.

Soon enough a couple of employees left the company, while some others were updating their resumes on job portals. One team member Fakruddin was seen everyday looking for job vacancies in newspapers.

I found it taxing to spend hours doing the soul-sucking work for a pittance, without much incentive. One day, on a Friday, I went outside the office compound and brought back a small bottle of vodka in my office bag. The working time was divided in shifts. The day shift people worked from 9am to 5pm while many, including me, worked in the evening shift from 2pm to 10pm in the night. I sat there working till the day-shift employees left the office. Now there were not many employees left. All girls also left. I emptied the vodka bottle in my water bottle. No one could guess it as vodka as it had no colour. Then I went on to slowly sip vodka from my water bottle. It made me feel better and working hard was easier then. In the back of my mind I was aware that I could get fired instantly if management knew what I was up to.

After that, I drank vodka from my water bottle, following the same process, whenever I felt bogged down by work. Luckily I never got caught!

Things were getting worse in the company fast. No one was feeling motivated enough to work hard as there were hardly any incentives to work for. Saurabh fired fifteen people for not achieving the impossible targets. Around twenty members of the staff left for greener pastures.

One day Supriya Sharma came to me. I kept looking at my computer screen while working. She looked at my computer screen and then at me.

"Hi Amit, how are you?" She asked trying to attract my attention.

"Hi, I am fine," I replied without looking at her.

"Hi Amit, can't you see a girl wants to talk to you?" She said with a feigned irritation.

I stopped work to look upto her face and smiled.

"Ok, so, how are the things with you?" I asked.

"I am not feeling good these days," she said.

"What has happened?" I asked.

"May parents are forcing me to marry a boy, a software engineer," she said.

I was surprised that she was letting me know this personal matter. She had talked to me several times in the past, but those were casual small talks. We were not close enough to share personal matters like that, I felt.

"I guess you have a boyfriend. That's why you don't want to marry that software guy? Right?" I asked.

"Yes. I love him too much to leave him," she said.

"So, what's wrong with your boyfriend? Can't you convince your parents?" I asked her.

"Well, he doesn't earn much. My parents are looking for a well-earning boy. I tried to convince them that even he will also earn much very soon, without success. They think the software guy can earn a lot and is soon likely to be sent to the US by his company," she said. I was impressed by her frankness.

"Can you live without your boyfriend?" I asked.

"No. I don't think so. I have known him for last ten years," she said. I didn't know what to say to her. I just tried to make a sympathetic face. She looked relived and went away soon.

One day Saurabh called for me. I went inside his cabin with nervousness. He was dressed neatly in a blue suit. He looked up at me and signaled me to sit on a chair.

"Amit, you used to perform quite well initially. What has happened now? I can't take these results from you. You must shape up. Now go and work," he said curtly and then got busy in his work.

"Ok, sir," all I could say and slowly left his cabin. I knew it was a bad sign for me. I wanted to leave the company before I was asked to do so.

I started to search for a new job seriously. I couldn't stand the mind-numbing work along with a punishing boss. Only fifty people were left in our team.

I got a call from Travel Times, a travel trade magazine based at Jungpura in South Delhi. The company was smaller as compared to Softdata and had its office in a basement. After 1st round of written test and 2nd round of interview I got the job offer. I was sure to get the job mostly due to the fact that the person in charge of recruitment was a young lady who seemed to like my face. My experience was that HR persons mostly hired persons of their opposite sex. It's a natural bias which is hard to beat. One of my friends had seen an extreme scenario. In the past the male boss hired staff that included both men and women. After he hired a lady as HR executive, the company never saw another female staff. She made it sure that only young men were selected. I had read a research report that showed that if the HR person was a lady then a beautiful young woman had a slim chance of getting a job in that company, due to the good old jealousy women feel for each other.

The job profile at Travel Times included working as a travel journalist-cum-editor. It sounded better than the current mind-numbing work that made one feel like an insignificant cog in a big wheel.

By the time I went to Travel Times for the final round of interview, the receptionist of the office knew me by face. I came quite early on that day.

"Sir, can you please sit at my seat for just a couple of minutes. I am just coming back in a minute," the lady receptionist requested me. It's difficult to turn down a request made by an attractive young lady, I tell you. I sat on the reception reluctantly. I saw the lady go out of the office.

I sat there for half an hour feeling amused, and answered several job candidates who came to the reception 'to ask something' that 'I'm not the receptionist, I've just come for an interview'. The lady apologized profusely when she came back.

Interestingly, there was another vacancy of similar profile at the travel journal. I called Suraj to inquire if he was interested in the job. He was keen to get rid of Romila and move on in life. He applied for the position and got the job. We both were scheduled to join the company on the same date. I was looking forward to work together with Suraj once again, the fourth time.

On my last day at Softdata, I heard the news that Saurabh had resigned and was going to join a rival company located across the road, after ruining the work atmosphere here.

Surpriya looked sad and disturbed when I saw her on my last day at Softdata. A month later I heard that she left both her boyfriend and the country to go to the United States with the software engineer, now her husband.

❑

Travel Times

I changed the job hoping for better work conditions and a better boss. Oh boy, I was hugely mistaken! The new boss Ajit Singhal was an angry old man. He had this habit of shouting at the top of his lungs. He was a tall, fair-skinned man, always clean-shaven and dressed in a suit. His face somehow reminded me of the face of 'Dracula' that I had seen on a book cover long back. This control freak was manipulative, sharp and cruel. And he wanted respect without actually deserving it.

One peculiar habit of Singhal was that he was very reluctant to give any leave to the staff. He always feared that they would go for job interviews. If any staff asked for leave due to a medical reason he had his stock of medicine to prescribe to him. Once a member of the staff called him to ask for a leave due to fever. Singhal asked him to come to the office to work and also take medicine for fever.

Singhal was so much averse to granting leaves that one member of the staff had to resort to a full-blown drama for leaves. He made a fake wedding invitation card for getting a week-long leave. No one from the office was supposed to attend his marriage as the venue was in a remote small town in the North East. Singhal never knew about the trick.

I got a taste of the new boss Ajit Singhal on the second day itself. I was busy in work when he entered the office. I was called in to the big cabin of the boss.

"Why didn't you greet me when I entered the office?" Singhal asked me. I was shocked as I was asked this question for the first time in my life. No boss ever made a big issue out of it.

"Sir..sir..I was busy in work. Didn't notice your arrival," I tried to string together a reply.

"Shut up! This is not a good excuse. Never forget that in future. Now go away!" Singhal shouted.

It was humiliating! Being shouted at a stupid excuse!

After some time I was called into his cabin again.

"Amit, why did you leave the office at 7pm?" Singhal asked. I was surprised at the question. The HR person had told me that the official time was 9am to 5pm. Finding some people still working, I left the office a bit late at 7pm on my first day of the new job.

"I'm sorry sir. I will try to leave the office on time at 5pm sharp," I said politely.

"I mean why did you leave so early? Didn't you notice that the people were working at that time?" Singhal shouted, clearly not mused at my answer.

"Sir, the official time is 9am to 5pm," I said.

"Shut up! The office coming time is 9am. But there is no fixed time for leaving the office. You have to leave office only when I will permit you. Understand? Go and work now!" he thundered.

I was speechless! What a rule this old asshole had created

to suit his convenience and eccentricities! Sadism was running deep in his blood, I thought. I knew that childhood abuse led people to become criminals and abusers in adulthood. He must have been abused and tortured in childhood or just born insane, I thought.

I soon realized I was at a wrong place. The company had a very high attrition rate. Most of the employees left the company within two months of joining. Some left within a week. There was just one employee who was working there for more than a year. His name was Prateek. He had a round-shaped body and a techie mind. The moustached man with a wicked smile was immune to Singhal's tantrums.

"I can't work here for long," Suraj said, looking equally disappointed.

"Me too," I replied.

"We need to come up with a good business plan of our own before we are screwed anymore," I added.

I started to think about various business plans. One fine day I emailed a business plan for starting an online travel agency to many people who had previously invested in startups. Five day later I got a call from one investor.

"Hi, Amit. I am Chetan Bajaj from Fast Venture Capital. I got your email about online travel idea. I want to discuss it in details. Can you please come over to my office tomorrow at 11 am?" he said.

I was surprised to get the call form Chetan, a high-profile investor of the country. Suraj had given me an idea that getting a venture capital was very difficult. I was very excited about the meeting.

"Thanks. Surely I will be there tomorrow," I said enthusiastically.

I asked for a half day leave from Singhal on pretext of going to the railway station to receive my parents. The next day I rose up early and prepared my dialogues to deliver before the high-profile venture capitalist.

I wore formal dress with a tie to present myself well in front of the investor.

I was impressed with the clean and sparsely decorated office of Mr Bajaj. I was asked to enter Chetan's cabin after waiting for him at the reception for few minutes. My Bajaj was a dashing young man with education from high-profile institutions like Harvard and IIM-Ahmedabad.

"Hi Amit, sit. How are you?' He asked me with a smile after shaking my hand.

"I'm fine," I said while sitting on a chair.

"So, you would like tea or coffee?" He asked politely.

"Thanks. I want coffee," I said with hesitation. He dialed his office phone to order coffee for me.

"I saw your business plan. I think India is now getting ready as an e-commerce market. I am very much interested in your plan. Do you have a business partner?" He asked me.

"Yes, Suraj is my business partner. If we get funding for our business we will work together," I said. I named Suraj knowing well that he would be very happy to work together with me in a new venture of our own.

"So, what about your education? It's not mentioned in your business plan. Are you from IIM or from a foreign university?" He asked me. I was surprised at his question.

"I am not from IIM or from any foreign university," I said.

"What? Then from IIT?" He was now looking disappointed.

"No," I said.

"Then have you studied in Uttar Pradesh?" He asked me.

"Yes," I replied. My answer surely disappointed him. He looked unhappy. He invited me for the discussion, expecting me to have passed out from a high-profile educational institution.

"Do you have a car?" He asked me. This question really bowled me over! What's the relation between starting a business and owning a car?

"No, I have a bike," I said.

Now he looked visibly angry as if I had wasted his precious time.

"Thanks. You can go now," he said curtly. I was surprised at this abrupt end of the conversation. I also felt sorry for displeasing him with my educational background.

I walked out of his cabin with hesitation. He still looked upset. I saw his office peon bringing a cup of coffee in a tray. It was too late.

I kept wondering where I went wrong in my conversation with Mr. Chetan. I also felt guilty for making him upset. Later I realized he was upset as I didn't belong to an elite educational institute. He felt proud in investing money in ventures started by guys from either IIM or with a foreign degree. He was also disappointed as I didn't belong to a rich family and didn't own a car. In his eyes only a small number of rich Indians were qualified to start a business.

I and Suraj realized that we had a lot of opportunities to learn new things if we survived with Singhal. Due to the high attrition rate we got to do work outside of our job profile, though officially we were journalists.

The only good thing about the new office was Swati, a spunky and confident girl in the editorial department. I noticed her the first day itself. She wore a *salwar-kameez* and looked like a traditional Indian girl. She was not at all affected by Singhal's attitude or bad tempers. Born and brought up in Delhi, she was a resident of Lajpat Nagar. She used to come to the office late and go home early. Surprisingly, Singhal was easy on her.

Swati left the job within two weeks after I joined the company. Before that we hit it off well and we exchanged mobile phone numbers. She sent me occasional sms containing random jokes after she left the office. I replied with similar types of jokes forwarded by my friends.

On that day, the moment I reached office I heard Singhal shouting at Prateek. I silently came and sat on my seat and tried to look busy in work.

"What is the matter? Why the boss was shouting at you?" Suraj asked Prateek after Singhal went into his cabin.

"He is angry because my shirt is dirty," Prateek said deadpan.

"What the hell! It's none of his business!" I protested.

"May be he was angry about something else, and found an easy vent," Suraj tried to figure it out.

"You are right," I agreed.

The next day Prateek was absent. Singhal was curious to know the reason. He called him at least ten times and got no response. When Prateek came the next day Singhal confronted him in the morning.

"Prateek, why were you absent yesterday?" Singhal wanted an explanation.

"Sir, I was washing my shirt," Prateek replied.

"What the hell! You can't spend the whole day washing a shirt. I called you so many times. Where was your mobile phone?" Singhal shouted at top of his lung.

"I lost my phone while returning back home the last day," Prateek said.

"Prateek, don't feed me all this crap. I know you are lying," Singhal was now really angry.

"Sir, I really lost my mobile phone. Here is the new SIM card I got from the telecom company," Prateek said meekly and pulled out a SIM card from his pocket.

Singhal looked confused and was trying to read face of Prateek. Then he went inside his cabin in a huff.

We gave smile to Prateek. He smiled back.

"You must be feeding him lies?" asked Suraj.

"Yes. I went for a job interview yesterday. I am totally sick of him," Prateek whispered. We had a good laugh.

Singhal had this habit of giving too much work to staff and forgetting them all later. In my case he kept giving me new work, even before I got time to finish the previous ones.

Thankfuily, most of the times he forgot the previously given work, otherwise I would have been torn apart due to a heavy workload.

The old-timer of the company, the programmer Prateek had perfected the art of handling Singhal. He used to spend 80% of office time researching about software and IT related topics, not related to the official work. Whenever Singhal asked him about what he was doing, this used to be his trademark reply, "I am searching for an anti-virus to tackle the latest dangerous virus that has attacked our office systems." Singhal used to fall for this excuse every time, as he believed Prateek was good at technology. He himself was technically challenged.

We saw recruitments going on almost throughout the year. One day when I was sitting in the cabin of Singhal for some discussion, a young man wearing a formal dress and a black tie entered the room obviously for being interviewed for a job. He spotted Singhal's pet Goldy, a dark black dog of bullmastiff breed sitting in the cabin. Goldy was a darling of Singhal and he used to take him along to the office and his cabin. The beautiful animal was generally nice in the office.

The candidate was visibly scared of Goldy. He looked unsettled and began to sweat.

"Sit down," ordered Singhal to the young man.

The candidate kept staring at Goldy.

"Sir, you first take this dog away," he requested with a mix of politeness and fear.

Suddenly Singhal went into a rage.

"How dare you call him a dog? He is not a dog. He is Goldy, my son!" Singhal shouted.

The candidate looked even more scared of both the dog and the master. He was visibly shaking out of fear.

"Goldy will not go anywhere else. Either you sit on the chair or go away but he will not move anywhere," he said waving his finger at the young man.

With eyes wide open and face showing intense fear, the young chap silently turned back and went out of the office. I was about to burst into a laughter, but controlled myself fearing another outburst by the boss.

Singhal slowly composed himself. He spotted his wife coming to the office. He turned to the pet dog and said "look Goldy, your mom is coming!"

Hearing this, Goldy ran out of the cabin, went upto Mrs. Singhal and jumped on her to show his affection and loyalty. The tail wagging furiously and the front legs on her shoulder. Mrs. Singhal was gladly patting him.

"The next," Singhal shouted sitting in his cabin. The next candidate for the job was sent inside.

A lanky young man sporting a thin moustache entered the room. He wore black pant and a blue shirt with a mismatched yellow-colored tie. The bespectacled man had well-combed black hair. He looked nervous.

"What's your name?" asked Singhal.

"Sir, Sharad Kumar," he replied politely while sitting on the chair.

Singhal looked into the bundle of resumes sitting on his table. Finally, he found out Sharad's bio-data.

"So, how was the day?" Singhal said with a fake smile looking up at the young candidate.

"Sir, today is Wednesday," Sharad replied. I guessed his English language was a bit poor. Singhal smiled on his answer.

"I mean did you spend your day nicely?' Singhal said.

"Yes sir," Sharad said.

"So, gentleman, say something about yourself and your life," Singhal said.

"I am Sharad Kumar married with two daughters," he said. Married his own daughters? I first wondered, and then realized he structured his sentence rather awkwardly.

"Go on," Singhal said.

"I have 2 months of work experience in marketing," the candidate said and became silent.

Singhal asked him, "Twenty seven years of life and this is all you have to say about yourself?"

"What will you do if I keep talking?" Sharad asked innocently. The simple question stunned both Singhal and me.

"Are you mobile?" asked Singhal.

"Yes, I have a mobile phone," said Sharad with a visible pride.

"No. I mean do you have a vehicle of your own? You may need it for marketing work," said Singhal.

"Yes. I have a bike," he replied.

"Ok. Tell me more about your family. What does your father do?" asked Singhal.

"He is a film distributor in Bhopal," replied Sharad.

"Film distributor? Interesting! Can I get a film role?" asked Singhal smiling, surprising me with his uncharacteristic fun mood. Maybe he was bored of taking many interviews.

Sharad looked dumbfounded.

"Tell me, can I get a film role with the help of your father? I fancy becoming a film actor," Singhal asked with tongue in cheek.

"You won't like to work in films distributed by my father," the candidate said calmly.

"Don't worry about it! I can work in any kind of film - action, romance or thriller," Singhal said smiling.

"My father distributes adult films, those shown in morning shows in small towns," Sharad said with a tinge of disappointment. I felt like laughing loudly, but controlled myself.

Singhal turned red with embarrassment. I didn't know why I felt so good to see him embarrassed.

Singhal said, "Ok. Nice to talk to you! You can go now. We'll let you know if we shortlist you. Just give me your email address. It's not mentioned in your resume."

"My email is sharadbhopal@gmail.com. The user ID is sharadbhopal and the password is premnagar," Sharad answered with a poker face.

This time I couldn't help laughing. Sharad looked at my face with amusement. The poor guy didn't know that giving his email password was a silly thing to do.

❑

Swati

Every dog has his days. I got a call from Swati.

"Hi Amit, how are you?" She asked me on the phone.

"I am just ok. Nothing much. How are you? Working in which company?" I asked.

"I'm not working these days. Don't feel like doing that. So, just sitting and watching TV," she replied.

"Sitting at home? Don't you want to make your career?" I was surprised.

"See, I am under no pressure to work. My father earns enough. He is a senior executive working for Maruti, an automobile company. I will join a company once I feel like doing that," she replied.

"You're lucky. We've to work our asses off to feed ourselves," I said.

"So, how do you like the new job," she asked.

"Singhal is really mean. He keeps shouting at any pretext. The only happy face in the entire office is that of Goldy's," I chuckled.

"He loves him more than his own son," she said.

"Does he have a son?" I asked.

"Yes, and a daughter too. Though Singhal doesn't seem to have a good relationship with his son," she revealed.

"I see. It's difficult to live with bad tempers of Singhal," I said.

"See Amit. I forgot to tell you that I need a new email account. The Internet connection at my home is having an issue. Can you create one for me?" she asked.

"Of course," I said.

"So, create a new account on Yahoo with my name as user ID and February as the password, and sms the details to me," she instructed.

"I will create one for you, but I will give you only when you meet me in person," I said with a smile. I think it was boredom of my life that made me say so.

"Oh, so you want to meet me. Let me check. I can spare time on the coming Sunday. Is it ok for you?" She asked.

"Ok," I said. We ended the call after some more small talk. I narrated the case of the candidate and the pet dog to her. She was laughing on hearing this.

I was elated but careful at the same time. I was looking forward to meet her. I didn't want to suffer another heart-break. I had not even got over Shruti completely. She still used to come in my dreams. Whenever I listened to the songs of the film *Fanaa* I got reminded of her. Shruti had come in my life too late. I hope I was not late in the life of Swati.

It was Sunday and I got ready for meeting with Swati. I put on my best casual clothes to create a good impression on her.

It was a nice morning of the spring season. The weather was cool, and my mood upbeat.

Swati was waiting for me near Satyam cineplex at Nehru Place. The morning sun was kissing her face. She was looking gorgeous. Cool breeze was playing with her hair. She looked a bit shy when she saw me.

We started with usual pleasantries. She sat quite close to me. I was feeling the heat of her body. My head was filling up with romantic thoughts. She was also in a playful mood.

We had burgers and coffee at McDonald's and then went to the Lodhi Garden. Going to the garden was my plan. I had heard it was a nice place for a date.

Sitting near a pond at the Lodhi Garden was so pleasant. It seemed surreal. I held her hands on the pretext of reading her palm. She didn't resist.

"You know Laali was feeling hungry yesterday and I fed her milk," she informed me.

"Why? Can't she eat herself," I asked her.

"She can't. She's a bitch in our street," she said.

"Oh, sorry! I thought it was your sister," I said and gave a laugh.

"She's very sweet and cute. I have seen her right from her childhood. I am worried that she's got weaker now," she said. I was touched to see her love for a street dog.

It was a nice meeting with her. I proposed to meet the upcoming Sunday as well, and she accepted. She let me know that on 15th February fell her birthday. We were supposed to meet on 16th February. Interestingly, I forgot to give her details of her new email account that I later sent to her though an sms.

I was upbeat throughout the week. Even Singhal seemed less sadistic in the week. On the Valentine's Day of 14th February I didn't feel like calling her. I feared she might feel offended. I gave her a call on 15th.

"Good morning. A very happy birthday to you," I said.

"Thank you," she said with chirpiness. Obviously, she was in a good mood.

"So, what are the plans for today?" I asked.

"Nothing much. I've got a new dress on my birthday. My mother is preparing some nice food and I'll cut birthday cake in the evening," she said.

"Good. So, what gift you want from me tomorrow?" I asked her.

"Nothing. Don't buy any gift for me," she said.

"Why?"

"Well, don't feel obliged to do it out of formality," she said.

"Ok," I said.

We met on the next day, again visiting the Lodhi Garden. Swati brought two pieces of her birthday cake.

"So, where is my birthday gift?" She asked me after I had a piece of her birthday cake.

"You said you wanted no gift?" I asked her, wiping my face.

"Don't you know that when a girl says no it means yes?" She said. I had a gut feeling about that, but it was refreshing to hear the same from a girl's mouth.

I gave out a loud laugh.

"Just close your eyes," I instructed her.

When she closed her both eyes, I put a pair of earrings in her hand. I had purchased the earrings for her the previous evening.

She was happy to see the small gift. I helped her wear that in her ears. I felt happy that she was happy with me. I was also surprised why Swati liked me and dated me when in the past I had mostly bad experiences. We parted without fixing another date.

In the night, I kept thinking about Swati. I could feel she liked me. I tried to analyze why she liked me. I guessed she was feeling bored at home and meeting me made her feel good. Obviously her liberal parents didn't stop her from meeting a boy. Another reason could be that I always made her laugh. She wanted to be entertained. As far I was concerned, I used to like any girl with beautiful eyes and a certain level of confidence. She had both.

At office, Prateek was now spending most of his office time searching for a new job. One morning Singhal noticed him reading a job supplement of a newspaper. He didn't say anything at the time.

Few days later Singhal caught Prateek searching for an opportunity on a job portal. The moment Prateek realized the boss watching his activity, he minimized the webpage. But it was too late.

Singhal was literally breathing down Prateek's neck. He took control of the computer mouse and opened the web page to confirm if it was a job portal indeed.

"Come in my cabin," He shouted at Prateek.

Singhal closed the door of the cabin after Prateek entered. Then the hell broke loose.

"How dare you do this? I need a bloody explanation!" Singhal shouted. "How dare you search for a job in the office hours using the office resources?" He demanded to know.

"I am sorry sir," Prateek said politely.

Singhal kept shouting at the top of his lung until he became tired. We could see Singhal's exaggerated facial and hand expressions through glass of his cabin. The old age must have mellowed him down a bit. I imagined he must have been a real devil in his young age.

Prateek came out of Singhal's cabin looking normal.

We had to go out for lunch as there was no canteen in the office. One day I was having lunch with Sooraj in a neighborhood restaurant. There was another table close to us where two boys and two girls were having their lunch. They were quite happy and noisy. Suddenly the ceiling fan fell down on their table with a loud noise. Everyone was shocked. The four people stood up from their chairs. The food was scattered all over the table. Thankfully, no one was hurt. The restaurant owner came over and ordered new plates for them casually, as if nothing had happened. We thanked our stars that the fan above our table was working well, and didn't fall.

One day we were shocked to see something unusual in the office. In full view of the office staff, Singhal slapped Shravan, the office peon. He was angry with him about a work done badly. Then he sent the peon out of the office for some other work. While coming back to his cabin he murmured 'son of a fool!'

Shravan was a long-serving employee of the company. He was a slim and a dark-skinned man from Jharkhand. He was living away from his family to earn a living.

We were shocked. Slapping and then abusing a poor man, with a family and kids, was a highly objectionable act. Singhal belonged to the old India when exploitation of the poor by the rich was considered normal. India has changed a lot in last many years, though not so much socially. The British should have taken Singhal along when they left India in 1947, I thought. One black Englishman was left behind to torture Indians.

I decided to take Swati to a movie after couple of meetings. I purchased two tickets of corner seats. I had selected a film that was badly produced and a flop, or at least I thought so. I was in no mood to watch the film.

Swati sat left to my seat. Thankfully, there were not many audiences in the hall. When the film started I slowly slipped my left hand on Swati's right hand. She didn't pull her hand back. I started to feel the heat in my body. I slowly started to massage her hand. All this while both of us kept looking at the film screen.

Swati's positive signals made me feel confident. I slowly turned my head in the left and kissed her on the cheek.

"What are you doing?" She whispered. I thanked God she didn't shout at me.

Two minutes later, I planted a light kiss on her lips. This time she was silent. My first kiss! This was a moment I had imagined in my mind for so long and it had finally turned into a reality! I tried to control my excitement.

"So, how was the week," I asked her.

"Let me watch the film," She said trying to look serious.

My mind started to wander once again. I was hardly interested in what was going on the screen. I was more interested in what was happening in my life at that moment.

I held her right hand in my hands and started to play with her fingers. She seemed to be enjoying that.

I gathered courage again and held her head in my both hands and put my lips on her lips. This time it was a deep kiss for full two minutes. Then I leaned back. I felt happy, relaxed and satisfied. I had read somewhere that kissing makes you relaxed and calms your nerves as some chemical is released in your brain. They were right, I thought.

"You are naughty. It is not done," she said.

"It's all your fault," I replied.

"How come!" She was surprised.

"You made me do it. It's because of your influence on me that I could not control myself," I came up with an explanation.

"You don't know how to kiss," I teased her.

"I can see through your smartness. You want me to kiss you. Right? I won't do that," she smiled.

"The next time I will teach you how to give a French kiss," I said.

"A girl like me should not kiss a boy," she said.

"Why?" I asked.

"According to the Indian culture we should not do that," she explained.

"What is the Indian culture? Have you seen a Khajuraho temple? Is it a part of the Indian culture or not?" I asked.

She looked puzzled.

"The Indian culture used to be permissive in old days. It was only after the foreign invasions that the Indian society became suppressive." I tried to take benefit of my little knowledge of the history.

"But they say that an Indian girl does not kiss a man before her marriage. That is why some people protest Valentine's Day," she said.

"Who says so? The people who know the least about the Indian culture shout the loudest about it. The same kind of people have turned India from the peaceful land of Kamasutra and Khajuraho into a violent society facing riots and anarchy," I said. I thought the reasoning went over her head.

"In any case, kissing a person you love is not bad at all," I added, appealing to her tender feelings.

"Excuse me. I don't love you yet. You are just a friend," she said. I gave a laugh.

Suddenly I heard a voice, "Kindly watch the film silently. We're getting disturbed." I turned my head backwards to see a white foreigner lady making the request standing in the back row.

"Ok, sorry." I all could say. She went back to her seat, away from our seat. I just had my first kiss and all this lady was interested in was this stupid film! We started to talk quite slowly. After some time the lady again came to request us to be silent. What a nag! It seemed she was focusing on hearing to us instead of watching the film. She was sitting far away from us and I wondered how we were disturbing her. Anyway, I didn't want to create a scene with a lady. I had thought that it was a flop film no one wanted to see, and here was a lady hell bent on watching it too much peacefully. The film was *Michael Clayton*, starring George Clooney. I decided never to watch an English film with Swati, at least not one starring George Clooney.

We parted without fixing a date for the next meeting.

I could not sleep the whole night. It was a big day for me.

My first kiss! I had a long-cherished dream of having a stable girlfriend who I could kiss any time I wished.

Suraj was not happy. One day he revealed new developments in his life.

"Parents are completely against my marriage to Ritu," he said.

"So bad! Fuck the caste system. It's all bullshit and a social evil," I said trying to sympathize with him.

"Ritu has given me an ultimatum. Either I marry her in two months or she will leave me," he informed me. Poor boy! He was screwed, I thought.

"So, what you have decided?" I wanted to know.

"I can't leave my parents. I am their only son," he said. "I don't want to leave Ritu either," he revealed.

We decided to meet the next weekend at my place and also invite Shantanu Basu and Satish.

We set the weekend tryst on Sunday. Drinks and snacks were arranged. Suraj and Satish reached my flat at the scheduled time. Shantanu didn't come on time. I got a call from him the moment I was thinking about giving him a call.

"Hi Shantanu, where are you? Everyone is already here," I said.

"Amit, kindly help me. I am surrounded by dogs in the street leading up to your house," Shantanu said fearfully.

"Hey just ignore them. Don't look at them," I said.

"But they're looking at me," he said.

"Ok, I am coming. Be there," I assured him.

I went out of the flat to see him staring at three barking dogs. I came close to him.

"See they're barking. They can bite me," Shantanu said with fear.

"Shut up! Just look at me and talk to me, and pretend that dogs don't exist," I told him. Shantanu tried hard to ignore dogs.

I took his hand and brought him to my flat.

"Dogs are like bad bosses. The more you are fearful of them the more they will bark at you," Suraj tried to reason with Shantanu when he reached my house. Though, he was too fearful to understand the reasoning.

"I have heard you got a new girlfriend, Amit. I am happy for you," said Satish changing the topic.

"Nothing. She's just a friend," I replied shyly. They guessed looking at my face that I was happy about it.

"So, how are your hot models?" I teased Satish.

"He has been warned by Romila against watching porn in the office hours," Shantanu informed us.

"So sad! It was the only reason for his survival," I said. We all laughed.

"I came to know about your troubles," Shantanu told Suraj.

"It's difficult to change an age-old mindset," Satish said. Shantanu nodded his head in agreement.

"Psychologically speaking, it's a revenge parents take for being forced to marry against their will by their parents. So, they in turn impose their wishes on their sons and daughters. Thus, this cycle of suppression goes on generations after generations," I reasoned.

"How can you say so? Parents always think better for their children," Shantanu said.

"Yes. But they don't always do good things for their children. Just read newspapers to know the truth. So many students commit suicide under tremulous pressure to succeed in a particular exam to satisfy ego of their parents. Most parents force their kids to achieve dreams they themselves failed to achieve. It's all unfair. And look at Suraj's case. Do you really think his parents are doing a good thing to him? Don't become blind," I said. "Forced marriages are rampant in many parts of India. We never realize that because we are so much used to it right from our childhood," I added.

"Amit has a point," Suraj said.

"You maybe right, Amit. Though I am surprised how you can say these things? Don't you love your parents?" Shantanu argued.

"I love my parents. But it doesn't mean that I become blind and refuse to see the reality," I said firmly.

"Ok. So, what you have decided, Suraj?" Shantanu asked Suraj.

"I will still try to convince my parents. If they don't agree then finally I may have to break up with Ritu," Suraj replied.

I felt bad for Suraj. I didn't know that something similar was coming my way too.

❑

Arranged Drama

My parents seemed ready to get me married. They had already sent to me photos of couple of girls in the past. I had said no to all the proposals. Initially, I felt flattered to know that some girls wanted to marry me. Later I realized that it was not me but my job. The desperate fathers of girls could marry their daughters to any idiot with a job. And I was never chosen by any of the girls in the photos, but by their old fathers, and random relatives. That's how most marriages are arranged in our country.

In fact I was not ready for the institution called marriage. I found the tradition of arranged marriages rather weird. How could you decide to spend your life with a person you didn't even know well?

One day I got a call from my father. He wanted me to see a girl for marriage.

My parents were coming to make me see a girl in Delhi. Though, I was enjoying my romance with Swati and didn't want any disturbance.

In fact, I had not forgotten even Shruti. One night after drinking a couple of pegs, I began to miss Shruti. Instantly I wrote a long email to her. In the sentimental email I wrote about how I missed her, and how I wished I had met her before she got engaged. I was neither expecting a reply, nor I got one.

After his arrival in Delhi, my father showed me a photo of the girl. She was not my type. I said no to parents. But my father was determined to take me to the girl's home to see her. My mother said we would go to see some other girl, though I had a gut feeling she was lying.

A friend of my father had arranged this match-making event. He went along with us to the girl's house. It's curious how many people in small towns and villages spent almost half of their life in arranging matches, and working as brokers between families of prospective brides and grooms. We all dressed up for the occasion. I wanted to wear something casual, but the parents made me wear a suit.

On our arrival to the girl's house, we were made to feel welcomed. I was embarrassed, as well as amused, to be part of this unique match-making event. It all seemed so filmi to me. The moment I saw the girl I knew my mother was lying indeed. It was the same girl in the photo. She was looking traditional. I didn't like the Indian tradition of suppressing women in the name of culture prevalent in many parts of the country. To me she looked like a suppressed woman, well-trained to serve the husband like an obedient maid. I was forming my opinions about her without properly knowing her. There was no time or opportunity to know her well, anyway. I wanted a life partner, not a housemaid, I thought.

We were served with a wide range of snacks and sweets. I didn't even want to eat sweets served there as I was determined to say no to the marriage proposal.

The girl came in the room. My mother asked her to sit beside me on the sofa. I was feeling uncomfortable sitting close to her. Even she was feeling uncomfortable playing with her fingers with the eyes looking down. I felt sorry for making her feel uncomfortable.

While talking to the girl's father, my father kept staring at the girl's face, as if to decide if the girl looked good enough to be accepted as a daughter-in-law.

"Don't feel shy. Have sweets. They are fresh," the elder brother of the girl, sitting on another sofa, told me.

"Ok, thanks," I said while picking up one small piece of the offerings.

My mother was alternatively looking at my father and the girl. Using eye contact she was exchanging notes with the father about the girl. My mother was an expert at saying a lot to my father using her stares and facial expressions. It was really entertaining to study their secret communications. I could guess they were satisfied with the girl.

"If you have any question ask her," my mother suggested to me, as if she had already accepted the girl as a daughter-in-law.

It was embarrassing to ask questions to a strange girl in front of known and unknown faces staring at me. Would asking a couple of obvious questions be enough to understand a person?

I declined to play the stupid game.

"I have nothing to ask. You do ask," I replied curtly.

My mother didn't ask anything. After taking tea and some sweets, she signaled my father that it was the time to go. At the parting time, mother of the girl forcibly pushed Rs. 1000 into my hand. I guessed it was considered auspicious to do so or maybe just a tradition. Anyway, I felt bad to take the money as I was unlikely to say yes to the marital alliance.

After returning from the girl's house, I looked amused at the whole experience.

"So, what is your decision? Should we say 'yes' to them?" My father asked me.

"I will decide and let you know later. I don't even know her properly. It's difficult for me to make a decision so soon," I said.

"Why didn't you ask questions to the girl to understand her," my mother wanted an explanation.

"How can you expect me to ask her stupid questions in front of people starting at me? There was no privacy for talking to her," I explained.

"I think we should have given him privacy for talking to the girl," my father told my mother.

"You should have asked her anyway. Everybody does so," she said while staring at me.

"I am not like everybody. It's stupid to ask a couple of questions and then decide to spend the rest of your life with a strange girl," I said.

"You should feel lucky that at least you got to see the girl before marriage. In our society people don't see the girl before the wedding day," she said.

"It's their life they may ruin it. It's my life I will do what I feel like," I said firmly.

"Do you mean all people going for arranged marriages are fools?" She asked with anger.

"I don't know about those people. I know that I don't feel comfortable marrying a girl without understanding her properly," I said.

"I told you not to let him go to Delhi. He has been spoilt. He has forgotten to respect our culture and follow our traditions," she told father.

I didn't know what to say.

"Things have changed, mother. People now-a-days first meet and understand each other and then marry," I tried to reason after few moments.

"This not our culture. This is Delhi's culture. You have to follow our culture," she said firmly.

"You can't force me to marry a girl against my wishes," I said and went into the other room to end the argument.

In a couple of days parents went back to Gorakhpur.

Ten days later I got a phone call from my father.

"So, should we say 'yes' to the girl's family?" He inquired.

"Say 'no' to them," I replied calmly.

"You were smiling when you came from the house of the girl? I guessed you were happy with this marital alliance?" He said.

"I may be smiling because I found it all rather ridiculous. I didn't ever mean to say yes," I said politely.

"This is not done. You have rejected many girls on one excuse or the other," he said sounding irritated.

"I'm sorry. I can't help it. I will marry only the girl I like," I replied calmly.

"And who is that girl?" He asked.

"I don't know. I'll let you know when I meet one," I said.

"Ok," he said and cut the phone call.

I could sense he was not happy.

Meanwhile Suraj's girlfriend had broken up with him. He loved his parents enough not to go against them, and had to pay the price. When he let me know about it he looked sad. I couldn't come up suitable words to express my sympathy. My recent experiences had taught me that getting your way with parents was not an easy task.

❑

I Love You

It's been ten days since I talked to Swati. Finally she gave me a call when I was enjoying coffee in the office sitting with Suraj.

"Hi, what's going on?" She asked.

"Nothing much on my side. You say?" I said

"Are you too busy these days?" She asked in a complaining tone.

"Busy, but not that much," I said with a smile.

"So, when you will spare time for me," She asked.

"Any day you want, ma'am," I replied.

"Let's meet on the coming Sunday," she proposed.

"Ok. The same place, the same time," I confirmed.

We met at Nehru Place and spent time at the Lodhi Garden once again. The meeting was less exciting compared to the last one. We kissed, but did nothing more as we were sitting in a public place frequented by even families. At a moment when we were kissing passionately we noticed a small kid staring at us.

We decided to meet the next Sunday too. This time I wanted to take her to a movie again. A cinema hall provided more romantic opportunity than an open public place, I had learnt.

I booked tickets of a forgettable flop film and was looking forward to the meeting.

This time I had to wait for her. She was late by thirty minutes.

I was lucky to have just couple of people in the cinema hall. Thank God, some producers make films for just lovers like us!

I felt confident enough to wrap my left arm around her shoulder. Wearing a black top and blue jeans, she was looking nice in my arm.

The perfume she used was driving me crazy slowly. I started to play with her hair using fingers of my left hand. I could feel the silky feel of her hair.

Five minutes into the film, I leaned towards her. She understood what I wanted to do and looked at me. I gave a slow and deep French kiss on her lips. I kept enjoying it keeping my eyes closed. She too seemed to enjoy this time. I could feel her heavy breaths. The kiss lasted for four minutes and it was making her breathless. After that I leaned back for some time. Then I kissed her right hand after taking it in my left hand.

After some time I started moving my fingers slowly on her hand, her arm, then shoulder, then neck, then cheek, then neck again. I could feel she was turning on. Now my fingers were slipping down towards her breasts.

"What are you doing?" She whispered into my ears.

"Nothing," I replied. I looked around. No one was watching us. A couple of audiences present in the hall were repenting their decision to watch the film, I could guess from the expression of their faces.

I stopped my operation for few minutes, then started all over again.

My right hand became active and it started to move towards her breast. Slowly I tried to slip my hand inside her bra. I pulled my hand back when she resisted. Few minutes later I tried once again. This time she didn't resist. After some time I pulled my hand out of her bra. Now I started to move my hand slowly all over her body. Due to a regular yoga regime, she had maintained her body well. I felt her hands, her breasts, her abdomen and her thighs. I felt incredibly turned on.

We kissed a couple of times more. I was feeling ecstatic. After the film ended, we went towards the exit door after other people left the hall. On the exit way on the staircase, I held Swati against the wall and started to kiss her. I thought no one was watching us as all had left. Suddenly I was distracted by an old couple coming out of the hall and giving us a dirty look. I guessed they must have discussed our behaviour later, as finding faults with the new generation is the favourite pastime of the old generation.

After coming out of the cinema hall, we sat at a bench.

"You kiss like a dog," she said.

What? Has she kissed a dog? What's the meaning of kissing like a dog? Was it a compliment or a criticism? I wondered.

"What do you mean by kissing like a dog?" I asked looking surprised.

"I mean it was a wet kiss," she said while smiling.

"Was it good or bad?" I teased her.

"It was nice," she said with the eyes looking downwards. Thank God, that's what I wanted to hear!

"So, how was your last week?" I asked her out of courtesy.

"Nice. I complained against a distant relative to an NGO," she whispered to me.

"About what?" I asked her with surprise.

"Don't tell anyone. They had hired a child labourer. I complained to the organization working for child care," she said with a smile.

"Really? Why did you do so?" I asked.

"See, using child labour is both immoral and illegal. I had to complain. The relative has a history of using child labour. In the past once I had discussed the issue with his family, but they laughed it off," she said.

"From where you got the phone number of the NGO?" I asked.

"From a newspaper," she said. I was secretly admiring her courage.

"Don't you feel fear?" I asked her.

"No. I had even got one computer training institute closed down two years back," she said.

"How come?" I was curious.

"The lady running the institute was rude and careless with students. She was charging much without teaching anything. Her institute was affiliated to a big training institute. I complained to the parent organization and they canceled the affiliation," she said calmly.

"Hey, you behave like a social worker," I teased her. She gave a laugh.

I gave Swati a parting hug when she was leaving for her home. I could see some random eyes looking at us.

The next morning I got an sms from Swati expressing her love for me. She signed off with these words 'i luv you, your Swati'.

I was pleasantly surprised to read the message. I couldn't believe it for few moments. I read it several times to confirm if they were indeed the magical words 'I luv you'. It was for the first time in my life that a girl had directly expressed her love for me. I was elated.

I didn't know what to reply. So, I simply wrote back 'thank you'.

❑

Kolkata

The next month was hectic for our company. We had to cover live annual conference of travel agents in Kolkata.

A couple of members of the staff, including me and Suraj, had to work for 21-22 hours a day for 20 days on a stretch, including 10 days spent in Delhi and the rest in Kolkata. Singhal had booked hotel rooms nearby the office. We used to work round the clock, except going to the hotel for taking a quick nap and getting fresh in just 2 hours.

A new staff Debajyoti Patnaik was finding it tough to keep working long hours in the office. He had just come from Orissa and he was not familiar with Singhal's way of functioning. One day after gathering courage he went to Singhal and said, "Sir, I want to request you something."

"Ok, tell me," Singhal said smilingly.

"Sir, I face difficulties working long hours. I can't work like this. Kindly permit me to leave early at 8 pm in the evening," he said politely.

Suddenly hell broke loose.

"How dare you say so? Do you think I'm a fool that I keep working hard? You get out of the office right now! You're just fired! Come next month and collect your due money," Singhal shouted. What an argument! Of course Singhal would work hard as it was his company and he was making loads of money out of it. In any case he was old and didn't need much sleep in the night. It wasn't the case with Debajyoti, a young man.

Singhal's reaction was not surprising, but what surprised us was the next move of Debajyoti. He went close to Singhal, who suddenly felt nervous. The chap politely touched feet of Singhal, turned back and went out of the office. We were speechless! What a great cultural difference between a small town and a metro city! In small towns they teach to respect elders in spite of everything, while a metro city can be ruthless to newcomers!

Babina, a Manipuri girl living in Delhi had just joined our office. She had also accompanied us on the Kolkata trip. Singhal, along with the marketing manager of the company Supriya Mehra, flew to Kolkata while he sent the staff by train. On the way to Kolkata on the Rajdhani Express, I had the upper berth, while Babina had the middle one. While lying on our seats, we kept chatting about random topics till the midnight. She depicted a nice picture of her home state. She complained about discrimination faced by her in Delhi due to her looks. She was mistaken for a foreigner several times in city. Blame the narrow-minded thinking of some people! To some residents in Delhi either you look like them or you are a foreigner. Even our hotel receptionist in Kolkata mistook Babina for a Chinese.

Our stay in Kolkata was quite busy. We had to cover annual conference of travel agents organized at the five star hotel ITC Sonar Bangla. Singhal stayed at the five star hotel while we were put up at a three star hotel. A taxi was booked for commuting between the two hotels during our stay in Kolkata.

One day when I was knocking Babina's hotel room suddenly

her door opened and I saw her standing topless in front of the mirror. Both of us felt embarrassed and I went back to wait for her at the lobby. Later she apologized for not closing the door properly before getting ready for the day's event.

My days were spent taking notes of the day's events and write news articles on the same. We used to work overnight to unsure the new issue of the magazine was out at the conference venue, to be distributed to the delegates. Suraj used to edit and proof-read the articles to make them print-worthy. The highlight of the day was usually the excellent food, served along with beer, by the hotel.

The most of the events were related to the problems faced by the industry. One day the central Minister of Tourism came and delivered a lecture promising the moon for the industry, obviously with no intention of fulfilling any of them.

One interesting event was a speech by noted motivational speaker Shiv Khera about how to become a better parent. With his well-prepared, emotionally charged lecture, he managed to impress many people, especially women. I could see some tearful eyes during the speech delivered in his trademark American accent. He was surrounded by lots of admirers after the event. What impressed me more was the fact that one could make a decent earning just by giving lectures to people! And here were we working our asses off just to make both ends meet!

One day I was writing a new story on a recent event sitting in the lobby of the hotel. Some colleagues were sitting around there too. A group of violin players were giving a live performance.

Suddenly I saw a bearded man coming to the violin players. All musicians got a picture clicked with the bearded man.

Out of boredom, my colleagues started to make guesses about the bearded man.

"I guess he is Aamir Khan," said Prateek.

"A bearded Aamir? He maybe Jackie Chan," said Babina.

"No. He is a twin brother of Jackie Chan separated in childhood at the Kumbh fair," Suraj said rather loudly.

The bearded man could hear us. He stared at us with a scowl on the face when Suraj passed the loud comment. We failed to recognize him.

Later it was revealed to us that it was film actor Jackie Shroff staying at the hotel for a promotional event of the Sony company.

On the second last day of the event a party was thrown by the organizers. Pop singer Usha Uthup gave a live performance. Suraj and I enjoyed free drinks and delicious food.

While I was in Kolkata I got a call from Swati. We chatted for some time. I promised to meet her after my return from the city.

"Ok, give me a kiss," I said before ending the phone call. By then, I had started to ask her for kisses at the end of phone calls.

"No," she said. I was surprised. What had happened? I wondered. I ended the call anyway. Later, she informed me that it was due to her father sitting in the same room.

On the last day of the event, I was in a hurry to arrange things up at ITC Sonar Bangla. Singhal was waiting for me at our three-star hotel. He gave me a call to look for Suraj and come back to the hotel. I kept looking for him at while I was feeling very hungry. I couldn't find time to take lunch earlier as I was busy in some work. Suraj's mobile number was busy. Suddenly I spotted a food counter at the same venue where the travel conference was held. I just picked up a plate and selected the choicest of dishes in the plate.

When I finished the food, I noticed that the food counter was for guests attending an event organized by cricketer Sourav Ganguly. I felt ashamed and went away from the venue as soon as possible, before someone could recognize me as a uninvited guest.

In the evening of the last day in Kolkata, Singhal organized a trip to tourist spots for the staff. We could see that Kolkata had retained its old time charm. Old buildings told stories of its past glory. I liked the Victoria Memorial for its grand looks and architecture. The Howrah Bridge had an old time charm. A boat ride on the river was immensely enjoyable.

"See, I am not as bad as you all think," Singhal told us after the trip, as if the organized trip was a huge favour done to us.

When the hotel bill of our stay was given to us we came to know that Babina consumed a good amount of whisky at the expense of the company, while we boys didn't do it fearing Singhal's wrath.

After coming back from Kolkata I came to know about a secret about Singhal.

The long-time serving office peon Shravan informed me that the 65 year old boss had an affair with our 45 year old marketing manager, Supriya Mehra. Ms. Supriya had joined the company when she was just 20 year old, fresh out of her graduation course from the University of Delhi, and she dedicated her life to both the company and Singhal. She remained unmarried and had been loyal to Singhal for more than two decades.

Shravan told me that the lovers used to meet secretly at the office warehouse located in a dingy lane of Paharganj. The warehouse had a sofa that could be unfolded to make into a bed. I didn't believe him at that time. Many months later I was forced to buy his story when I actually saw the sofa on my only visit to the warehouse. I suddenly got reminded of the lovers' weekly visit to the warehouse. They always returned happy after the visits, and remained in a good mood throughout the day.

Interestingly, Singhal was already married when Supriya joined his company. Now father of two, he managed to keep both his wife and the marketing manager happy. Shravan described me a fight between Singhal and his wife over Supriya. Then Singhal had saved the day by resorting to dramatics, hitting his head against the wall, and claiming that the company would be forced to close down without Supriya.

I felt bad for Surpriya as she was wasting her life for an old married man. If it was love then love could surely make women do crazy stuff, I thought. Now I could understand the reason behind her bad temper and tantrums that she used to throw regularly at us. Almost every day she used to find some excuse to shout at someone, mostly me. I had this gut feeling that if women didn't get married by the age of forty they became bad-tempered. After all, if you don't follow the dictates of the nature then it takes revenge in its own way.

Always clad in saris, Supriya used her charm for selling advertising space in the travel magazine. She had grown older by now and I found her a couple of times complaining about our competitors using scantily clad young girls for selling advertising spaces in their travel magazines. The old blood was finding it tough to complete against the young blood.

Sometime later, after one rare tiff with Singhal, I saw Supriya coming out of his cabin and saying, "Why did you hire me if you didn't like my face." "Just sit outside. I'll talk to you later. I am very busy now," replied Singhal. Supriya's words were revealing.

❑

Suraj's Marriage

One day Singhal entered the office smiling and replied happily to our greetings. It was unusual as normally he ignored greetings and looked in a bad mood while entering the office. Uncharacteristically, he treated us nicely the whole day. I was surprised about his sudden temperamental change. He gave us a treat of *samosa* and *jalebi* in the evening. Later it was revealed that it was the birthday of his dog, sorry, his son Goldy. Prateek joked in Singhal's office that it was more beneficial to be a dog than a man.

The Kolkata visit had made me more ambitious. I started to actively look for new business plans. I didn't want to work hard to make my boss rich. I deserved better things in my life, I felt. I had not forgotten unfair treatment at the hands of my ex-bosses. My first boss in Delhi had refused to give me a raise without any viable reason, while other staff got a handsome raise. Talk about abuse of power! It was humiliating. It's nowhere written in rulebooks that only ass-lickers should be given a raise or promotion.

"My marriage has been fixed. The date is 25th of the next month," Suraj informed me without showing any emotion, the moment I entered the office.

"What? With whom?" I questioned.

"With a girl in Lucknow. It's arranged," he let me know.

"Oh, are you ok with this? I mean are you ok with this kind of arranged marriage?" I asked him while sitting on a chair.

"I have no choice. I don't want to go against my parents. They have taken great pains to bring me up."

"Do you know the girl? Have you seen her?"

"No."

"What the hell! How can you marry a girl without even knowing her? At least make sure to see her personally," I said.

"You know that arranged marriages are a norm in India. You are a misfit in the Indian society, I am not," he said.

"Well, as a matter of fact, you are right. All I can do is wish you all the best for your marriage. Still make sure to see her once, just for the sake of it. A known devil is better than unknown one," I reasoned.

"Ok. But you can't judge a devil by her looks alone," he said. I nodded my head in agreement.

I didn't know that Indian societal norms were going to hit me soon.

I got a call from my father. He wanted me to agree to marry the girl I had seen some time back in Delhi.

"Papa, I have already told you I won't marry that girl," I reasoned.

"Look, I want no argument. Just see her photo again and make up your mind to marry her," my father said firmly.

"You can't force me to marry her. It's against my freedom to choose my life partner," I said.

"In our country, parents decide who you should marry, not you," he reasoned.

"Look father, I am not a kid any more. I am an adult and I have freedom to take major decisions of my life. With all respect due to you, I'm not a toy in your hand," I said. I guessed I must have sounded filmi and dramatic to him.

"You never listen to us. Even in your college days you never prepared for a government job or IIT," he said.

This had nothing to do with the marriage topic. However, I got reminded of the intense pressure I was under to take either competitive exam for a government job, or for IIT. I got reminded of how my mother made sarcastic remarks against me, comparing me to a friend's son who had got into an IIT.

"We have suffered all the pains in life to bring you up. I and your mother have made many sacrifices for you. You can't let us down like this. People in the society will make fun of me if you didn't agree with me. Stop all these arguments. Just do what I tell you. I'll call you again soon," he said in an emotionally charged tone.

I was in tears. I didn't expect this sort of behavior from my father.

The next day I shared with Suraj what had happened to me.

"You want to know? I am under intense pressure by parents to marry a girl of their choice," lamented.

"It was expected. Parents can't change their mind at this ripe age. They expect us to follow them without questioning," he said.

"My father called me yesterday and started emotionally

blackmailing me. He also complained that I didn't take any exam for a government job or IIT," I said.

"It's understandable. He is a government servant and he would like his son to follow the same path," he said calmly.

"See, I hate government jobs. Those jobs kill spirit of a man and make him just another corrupt person. People, will semi-feudal mentality, want to go into a government job for power and to make money out of corrupt practices. You will rarely find an honest government employee. My father keeps telling stories about his corrupt colleagues," I said.

"Well, in that case you may have tried to get into an IIT." Suraj said.

"Why should I prepare for an IIT, when I have no interest in engineering? I wonder how millions of young children in our country get emotionally tortured by their parents in the name of IIT. I always wanted to do things on my own and start my own company. Why should I join IIT?" I went into a monologue.

"But even today you are working hard to make Singhal rich. With an IIT degree you could have at least become a better-paid employee," Suraj reasoned.

"This is a temporary phase. It will pass. I will be running my own show one day. You don't need to have an IIT degree to do any remarkable thing in life. IIT is an obsession with only some middle class parents, who have failed to achieve anything remarkable in their own life. We all can become whatever we want to become. Though most people end up becoming just what they are expected to become by their parents and the society. But yes, trying to convince my parents about all these things was useless when I was a student," I said.

"I understand what you want to say. It's difficult to convince parents about these things," Suraj said.

"By the way, don't take me wrong. I was a good student in my student life. Though I was good in only subjects I was interested in, and never got the top marks because my focus was never on getting marks. The only real purpose of education can be inculcating the habit of critical thinking, not passing some damn examination! To be fair the best things we learn in life are all outside of classrooms," I said.

"But formal studies are also important," Suraj reasoned.

"Of course they are! They give us basic knowledge about the world and our own country. Though it's not everything. I feel bad when students kill themselves when they don't get excellent marks. Even Albert Einstein didn't get good marks in exams in his student life. Talking about Delhi, the city has many illiterate people running businesses with turnover of crores of rupees, and have people from IIT and business schools working under them," I said. "By the way, what you wanted to do in life during college days?" I asked Suraj.

"Well, in my case I wanted to become a journalist. After finishing a course in journalism from Lucknow, I came to Delhi and tried my luck with several newspapers and even TV channels also but no success. All I got was a chance to write crime stories in a *Manohar Kahaniyan* type of magazine. I later understood that to get a job in media you need contacts. Most of the media houses don't advertise job vacancies and recruit friends or relatives of existing employees," Suraj said.

"It's also a kind of corruption, when the deserving ones are jobless and the less-than-deserving are churning out mediocre work. Nepotism is a big problem in our country," I said, sympathizing with Suraj.

After this serious discussion we opened our desktops to work.

Some days later, my mother called me and tried to emotionally blackmail me.

"You know what? If you don't agree with your father, he will be left with no respect in our society. He won't be able to face any one," she reasoned, while crying on phone. I felt bad for her. I didn't want to make her cry ever. However, at the stake was my life. I needed to assert myself, I thought.

"I don't understand. What's the relation between my marriage with that girl and my father's social prestige?" I asked calmly.

"If you fulfill your father's desires then only he will maintain his respect in the society. You are well-educated, but it doesn't mean that you stop respecting your elders. You know Ramnath Mishra, our distant relative? He has earned so much money and respect in the society. Still he is traditional and his children follow his instructions," she said. Ramnath Mishra, a Chartered Accountant by training, was running an accountancy firm in Lucknow. He was rich and had contacts with the senior politicians and bureaucrats. He was well-respected by my relatives. I didn't have any personal contact with him. I had seen him only a couple of times at family gatherings on the occasion of some weddings.

"I'm not competing with the children of Mishraji. They can do whatever they feel like and I will do what I feel like. I was not born in this world to imitate behavior of children of a rich man," I said with visible irritation.

"Well, people have started saying that you have already chosen a girl in Delhi for marriage. That's why you have declined several marriage offers in the past," she said.

"I assure you there is nothing like that. In fact, I'm in no mood to marry as of now," I said.

"You can marry at the time of your convenience. Just say 'yes' to her and we will wait for the right time whenever you'll be ready to marry with her." She gave me an option.

"I'm sorry. I can't marry that girl. I will marry only that girl who I like. I am not too desperate to marry any girl," I said.

"She is fair, tall and belongs to a respected family. What's wrong with her?" She asked me.

"There is nothing wrong with her. She's just fine. But she is not my type," I said.

"What's your type?" She asked.

"I will let you know when I will meet someone," I said meekly trying to sound reasonable.

Out of anger, she cut off the phone call midway.

Later my parents organized a high-profile *puja* at home to ward off some evil which supposedly made me refuse their marriage proposal. Many relatives were invited on the occasion. Obviously, the only person making any benefit out of the superstitious mumbo-jumbo was the priest.

Suraj's wedding ceremony was nicely held. Shantanu and Satish along with me attended the event held in Lucknow. It was nice to meet my friends in a new place. We had enough of dancing and drinking. Suraj's face showed no expression during the entire event. May be he was just taking it as another formality. May be he had gone numb.

After some drinking and dancing we saw Suraj sitting on top of a mare. It's funny people continued this kind of tradition in the world of fast cars. The wedding party moved along with loud music and dancing. The narrow lane leading to the bride's house was not well lit. Many people crowding the alley made things worse.

Suddenly the mare tripped over a random road-side brick and lost balance and shook uncontrollably. Obviously, the groom didn't have practice of horse-riding. Suraj fell down in a road-side ditch. The people were shocked. The next thing I remembered was that Suraj was pulled out of the small ditch, with his clothes dirty in mud. New clothes were ordered and Suraj had to change his clothes by the side of the road. All this while most of revelers were unaware of what had just happened to the debonair groom.

❑

Romance

Swati invited me to visit her house when I came back from Lucknow. I was suspicious of her intensions this time. Her mother must be hearing wedding bells, I thought.

I got prepared to go to Swati's house. I prepared myself for facing her mother who might pose some uncomfortable questions to me. When I reached Swati's house I noticed her house was well-decorated. The cleanliness of the house was a much contrast to my flat, where clothes and objects are thrown here and there all over the place.

Swati cheerfully welcomed me. Dressed in a white top and grey skirt she looked pretty. She made me sit on a maroon-coloured sofa. I felt self-conscious sitting in her room. There was no trace of her mother till then.

"Mother has gone to meet my aunty. She may get back in a couple of hours," Swati said while offering a glass of water to me. She sat beside me on the sofa.

"Ok, and where is your father?" I asked her.

"In the office," she said. I felt relieved that both parents were not present at home. Now I was feeling more relaxed at her home. Only her younger sister Mona was at home.

"Where is your sister?" I asked.

"She is upstairs. May come back soon," she informed me with a smile.

Soon enough her sister came downstairs. She greeted me with a smile and then sat on a sofa opposite me. She switched on the TV and started watching a movie.

"We'll take lunch in an hour. So, what you want? What is your favorite dish?" She asked me.

"Anything. I'm not a foodie. Though, I like *matar-paneer* or *aloo-matar*," I said.

"Ok," she said thinking about the vegetables available in her kitchen.

"She's a big fan of Salman Khan. She can see any film of him, even a flop one," Swati said while talking about her sister.

"She is a teen. Must be liking his muscular body. The usual teen crush! It happens in her age," I said.

Mona gave me a stern look. I smiled.

"Now I should start preparing the food. You just sit and watch TV with Mona," Swati said and went inside the kitchen.

As expected Mona was watching a Salman Kahn movie.

To avoid boredom I started talking to her sister.

"So why you like only Salman Khan?" I asked her.

"He is a great actor," she said with a visible pride.

"Really? People say he can't act," I teased her.

"No. Those people don't know him well enough," she explained.

"Besides acting, what's good about him?" I asked.

"He has a great body and is very cute," she said with shyness.

I didn't want to waste my day with a Salman Khan fan.

I stood up and went into Swati's kitchen while calling out for her. She smiled when she saw me in the kitchen.

I could see her kitchen was well-organized with all stuff stocked well in boxes of various sizes with proper labels stuck to them. It was impressive compared to my own kitchen with all items scattered all over the place. It took me much efforts to find the right items at the right time.

"I'm impressed with your kitchen. It's well-organized," I complimented her.

"It's just ok. I know how to maintain my kitchen," she said with a visible pride.

"My kitchen is in a mess," I said, disappointed with my own mismanagement at home.

I could see she was preparing *poori* and *matar-paneer* for me. The smell of nice food was making me feel happy. I felt happy to see her working hard to prepare food of my choice. I went behind her and covered her in my arms and gave a peck on her cheek.

"What are you doing? Mona may come any time," she whispered to me.

"Let her come. We are care-free lovers. We don't care," I said.

"But you have never said 'I love you' to me," she said in a complaining tone.

"Everything is not said. Many things have to be understood," I said and gave her a kiss on her lips.

We were in a lip lock when I heard Mona calling out her sister's name. The romance ended abruptly. I went back to the drawing room.

"Why were you calling Swati?" I asked Mona.

"I was just checking if the food has been prepared or not. I'm feeling hungry," she said.

"Relax. It will be ready soon," I said sitting on the sofa. I was enjoying the smell of food coming into the drawing room.

Soon Swati came up with three plates. Mona also helped in bringing food from the kitchen.

I was enjoying delicious home-made food after a long time.

Swati took me to the second floor of her house. It had two large rooms. One room had a chair, a desktop on a table, and a large bed.

We sat on the bed while chatting about random things. Mona was downstairs still watching the Salman Khan movie.

Sitting on a bed made my heart go crazy. I grabbed Swati in my arms and gave her a deep kiss. Then I kissed her hands and thanked her for preparing good food for me. Just when I was kissing her neck I saw Mona standing near the desktop. She must have seen me kissing her sister, I suspected. I was embarrassed and pulled myself away from Swati. We had forgotten that the door was still open. What a stupid mistake!

Swati looked normal and stared to talk about random topics still sitting at the bed. Mona was opening the desktop, while sitting at the chair.

"So what did you do this week?" Swati asked me.

"Nothing much. I hate the boss. He keeps shouting at his staff," I said.

"How was the trip to Kolkata?" She asked me. I was talking to her but my mind was wandering somewhere else. I was feeling turned on sitting on a bed with her. Mona was busy with the computer. I was lying on bed with the help of a pillow. Swati was sitting facing me with her back to her sister.

"It was exciting. We worked very hard. I really enjoyed the free food and beer served at the five-star hotel, the event venue," I said.

"Did you bring something from Kolkata?" She asked me. I could see under her skirt. I spotted her thighs and panty from my vintage point.

"Sorry, the city had nothing special, which is not already sold in Delhi. There were many interesting programmes at the event. There was a lecture by motivational speaker Shiv Khera about how to become a better parent. We saw a live performance by pop singer Usha Uthup. We also spotted film actor Jackie Shroff without recognizing him," I said, while slowly moving my right-hand fingers towards her left thigh.

"You should have brought something as a memento," she said shyly. The touch of my fingers on her thigh was making her feel shy, I guessed.

"Sorry. I'll keep this thing in mind, when I visit another city the next time. On the last day we visited various tourist spots. The Victoria Memorial is a grand monument. I found most of the buildings in city were quite old. It's an old city, you know. A boat ride on the Hooghly river was relaxing. The sight of the Howrah Bridge made me feel nostalgic, as it has an old-world charm," I said slowly taking many pauses, while touching and feeling her smooth thighs under the skirt. I could feel she was turning on.

"Where did you stay in Kolkata?" Swati asked slowly, looking intoxicated. I knew she was asking questions just to show to her sister that we were having a normal conversation. She would have enjoyed the physical excitement silently otherwise. I was sure Mona had no clue what was going on here.

"The members of the staff were put up at a three-star hotel, while Singhal was staying at the five-star hotel, which was also the venue of the event," I said. Now my hand was touching her panty.

Suddenly, Swati's mobile phone rang. I pulled my hand from her skirt in a hurry. She picked the phone and talked for a couple of minutes. I guessed it was her mother.

"My mother is coming within half an hour," Swati said while putting down the phone on the bed.

"It will be better to go now," I said. I had already spent some nice time there. I didn't want to face her mother. I had a gut feeling that all mothers of young girls looked at young boys with suspicion.

"Why so soon? Wait for some time. Go after meeting my mother," she said.

"Sorry, I have some important work to do today. I will surely meet your mother the next time when I'll come here," I said while standing up.

Swati accompanied me to the main exit door.

"Thanks for the nice food. I'll come back here soon and meet your mother," I said.

She gave a parting kiss on my cheek.

I was worried about Mona seeing me and Swati in a compromising position. I guessed she must have seen me kissing Swati's neck. Two days later I got a call from Swati. After some random talk, I asked her about Mona, expecting to get some news.

"Mona told something about us to mother," Swati informed me.

"What? I think she saw me kissing you," I said sounding worried.

"Yes, she said something similar to her," she said in a relaxed tone.

"Didn't you feel worried? What your mother said?" I asked.

"She told me that Mona was saying something about us. Mother was not specific."

"So, what was your reply?"

"I told mother it was just that we were sitting on bed together. She looked convinced with my explanation," Swati said.

"Thank God. Your mother is really nice. Though, your sister is not so nice," I said.

❑

Love in the Air

One day, Shantanu called me to inform me about his plan for second marriage already finalized. The bride worked in the sales department of a leading English newspaper in Delhi. I was happy for him. The news deserved a party. He threw a party at my flat.

"It's a great news, Shantanu. Best wishes," Suraj congratulated Shantanu.

Shantanu was in a sober mood. He replied, "Thanks. I need these wishes."

"By the way, how is your married life?" Satish asked Suraj.

"Just fine! It didn't have much impact on me," he replied.

"Really? Marriage is supposed to change you. Isn't it so?" I asked.

"Not in my case," Suraj said.

Shantanu's wedding ceremony was held in Kolkata. We couldn't attend his wedding ceremony this time. Though, Suraj, I and Satish attended the reception held in Noida. This time the whole atmosphere was a bit subdued.

Swati called me after some days. She wanted to meet me. I proposed to meet at Nehru Place. She wanted me to visit her house. I gathered enough courage to visit her home once again.

I was fortunate once again. She was alone at home with her sister. Wearing a maroon top and black jeans, she looked beautiful as usual. I wanted to avoid intimacy with Swati but it was very difficult to control your natural instincts.

This time Swati prepared chicken curry and *poori* for me. It was delicious. I suspected she wanted to psychologically control me using her culinary art as a tool. Even while eating tasty food my mind was thinking of romance. After taking lunch, Mona started watching TV. I didn't want to discuss what she told her mother about me. I generally avoided talking to her. I had thought she was a kid and she proved me wrong with her actions. She was doing graduation and didn't have a boyfriend, Swati had informed me. I guessed it was sibling rivalry that made her complain to her mother about Swati and me.

Swati and I went to the second floor. We sat on the same large bed. Taking advantage of the privacy, I kissed Swati's hands. My heart was going wild. I hugged Swati tightly. Soon I was kissing her all over the body. After a deep kiss on lips, I put my hand on her breasts. She was turning on. I slowly slipped my hand inside her top. She didn't resist. Feeling encouraged, I tried to pull her top off.

"What are you doing? My sister may come any moment." She looked worried.

"What to do then? I feel like doing something," I said.

"Feel like doing what?" She asked shyly.

I smiled mischievously.

Swati stood up and went on to close the entry door.

"We will have to open the door the moment Mona comes upstairs," she warned me and sat on the bed.

"Why would she come upstairs?" I asked her while kissing her on the neck.

"She makes tea in the afternoon and serves to me too," she replied after giving me a kiss on the cheek.

My head was in a tizzy. I started to kiss her wildly, on the lips, on cheeks, on shoulder and on the neck. She pushed me down on the bed. She lied on me and started to kiss me on my face. I felt good that she took initiative. She pulled my T-shirt and vest off, and started to kiss me on the neck and the chest. It was an incredible experience to be kissed by her like that.

I sat up and tried to remove her top. Swati helped me in doing that. I removed her bra and now she was topless. I fondled her body and kissed all over.

I unzipped her jeans. It was tough to remove it. Why girls wear so tight jeans? Sensing my mood, Swati slowly removed her jeans and started to fold it properly.

"Stop folding the damn jeans. We don't have much time. Mona may come any time," I said.

"I washed and ironed it yesterday. It's so beautiful. Purchased it last month at Sarojini Nagar market," she said. I was not interested in the history of the jeans. I gave her a kiss on the lips, which is the best way to make women silent.

Now I was lying on top of her. I was exploring her entire body. After some time Swati pushed me on my back and lied on me. She helped me in removing my jeans. Her kisses and touches on my body made me go wild. Soon we became one. For the first time I realized women enjoy physical intimacy as much as men.

After half an hour, we sat up on the bed. It was a heavenly experience for me. Finally, I had lost something I was desperate to lose-my virginity! My head was feeling light as if some big burden was off my head.

We didn't get enough time to relish the moment. Mona was knocking at the door! Swati dressed up quite fast, within seconds. It was surprising as normally she took half an hour to dress up. Emergency can surely make people work fast.

I couldn't put up clothes that fast. After putting on my jeans I ran towards the washroom with my T-shirt and vest in hand. After locking the door of the washroom, I got properly dressed up and arranged my untidy hair. After few minutes I came out trying hard to look normal.

Swati was sitting with a cup of tea in her hand along with her sister. Her flushed face must have raised suspicion in the mind of her sister, I thought.

"Take tea. It's quite good," Swati said while trying to look normal. The tea was served with salty and crispy biscuits.

Soon Mona went downstairs.

"Was she suspicious?" I asked Swati.

"Not this time," she said.

"Ok. Did you enjoy that?" I asked her. Of course she enjoyed, but wanted to hear from her mouth.

"What?" She asked.

"You know what I mean?" I said with a smile.

"Yes," she whispered shyly.

"I liked that too. Today is one of the best days of my life," I said.

"Enough of dirty things! Let's go downstairs," she said.

We sat downstairs in the drawing room. Swati brought some snacks for me. We kissed again when she was sending me off at her door. I could see a certain spark in her eyes.

I felt so good the rest of the day. The next few days were the best days of my life. I had a certain feeling of peace and contentment never experienced in life. I realized why Osho wrote the book *From Sex to Superconsciousness.* The path to superconsciousness indeed goes through sex.

I realized I had become more emotionally attached to Swati now. In fact, I had not taken her seriously till then. Now I had started to have tender feelings for her. I had read somewhere that physical intimacy increases emotional attachment. Well, the writer was right.

Later, I became worried that we didn't use any protection. I repented not using that. I didn't want to put Swati in trouble.

Swati had subtly changed me, and I started to realize that. I remembered how she called me frequently and cared for my well-being, and how she was worried when I had got a minor cold. It's wonderful to be cared for! She used to give me undivided attention, a wonderful thing. Due to her insistence I also got rid of smoking. I felt that in my childhood, my mother couldn't give me enough attention as she had to care for my two brothers too. In fact I felt cared for in my childhood only till my younger brothers were born. After that they were pampered at my expense. It was unpleasant to think about your mother this way, but I couldn't help.

I was touched when one day Swati told me that she kept

records of important days of our relationship. She had noted down the day I met her, the day we went on a date, the day I kissed her, and the day I went to her house. It was nice to know that I was so much important for her.

Before meeting Swati, I was a self-centered person. Now, I had started to think about her and how she felt about certain things. I liked her eyes, her boldness and her caring nature. She used to make me feel good about myself. Maybe she took care of my feelings, or it's just that all girls behaved that way till they married their boyfriends. Nevertheless, I was quite happy and secure in her company. What I also liked about her was that she used to laugh at my jokes.

Some days later, I got a call from a lady, sounding like a middle-aged woman.

"Hello, Amit. How are you? I am Swati's mother."

"I'm fine. Thanks." I replied.

"So, what have you thought about it?"

"About what?"

"About marriage with Swati."

I was stunned. Of course I liked Swati. But I was not ready for commitment. We had never discussed about marriage. I was out of the blue.

"Well, I have not yet decided about my marriage," I replied with hesitation.

"So, when will you decide?" She wanted to know.

"I can't tell you right now."

"You do decide and let me know. Swati has told me that she will marry only you. She is not ready to marry any other guy.

We are concerned about her marriage," she said and ended the call after some formal small talk.

My head got into a tizzy. I didn't expect something like that.

In half an hour, I called Swati. After exchanging the usual pleasantries, I let her know about her mother's call to me.

"I know. They are putting pressure on me for marriage. I have told them I will marry only you," she replied with a smile.

"Well, I am not prepared for marriage yet. I have never thought about it yet," I replied.

"I'll wait for you. I want only a promise from you. I can wait for several years."

"But why you want to marry me?"

"Because I love you, *Shona*."

"I can't promise you anything. You are free to marry any person."

"No. I will marry you only. You make me feel good. You also take care of me," she said. I wondered when I took care of her.

"Ok. Then you wait. I can't promise you anything. My parents also want me to marry some other girl. I have said 'no' to them too," I replied and asked her, "tell me frankly, have you told everything about me to your mother?"

"Yes, most of things," she said calmly.

"Have you also told her that I kissed you, you stupid girl?" I asked with a fake anger.

"No. How can I say these things? Though, I am open to my mother and share all the things with her. She is the only person in the world, besides you, I can be myself with," she said.

I was surprised at that kind of relationship with mother. I remembered once my ex-colleague Priya told me that she shared with her mother everything related to boys in her school and college days. Once she took a love letter given by a boy in school to her mother. The poor boy didn't know who he was dealing with.

It was a sign of a healthy relationship to share things with parents. Here was I, not sharing anything with my parents. They never looked interested in my personal or professional matters anyway.

One day in the working hours when we were busy checking emails and sipping coffee, we saw a policeman come to the office. We were surprised to see Police in our office?

"Who is Ajit Singhal here?" He asked in a baritone. He was a fat, moustached man.

"He is our boss. He will come within half an hour," I replied.

"Ok, I want to meet him. Let him know I am waiting for him here," he said and sat on a chair at the reception.

We called Singhal to inform him. He soon came to the office.

"How are you? Is everything fine?" asked Singhal to the policeman. I was surprised to see the confidence of Singhal in front of a policeman looking out for him.

"Are you Singhal? A member of the staff of your company has complained to us that you have not given him his salary and also you are running your office in a residential area," the policemen said curtly. We, the staff, were happy sensing that Singhal would be in a trouble.

"Oh really? Let's come inside my cabin and chat," said Singhal without any sign of nervousness or worry.

Both Singhal and the policeman went inside the cabin. The office peon was ordered to send tea and snacks inside. Half an hour later, the policeman emerged out of the cabin holding hand of Singhal and laughing. He parted way with Singhal as if he was an old friend of his. We were surprised at the policeman's transformation from the angry young man to a friendly young man! It later emerged that an ex-peon of the company had complained to the police after getting fired without getting salary after an argument with Singhal. The policeman buried the matter after Singhal greased his palm.

I had not forgotten my tryst with Swati at her home. I was looking for another similar opportunity. I knew it was tougher as her mother was now more watchful about my moves. I remembered once Swati wanted to see my home. The only issue was that it was a rented accommodation and the landlord was an unpredictable jerk. I didn't know how he would react about me inviting a girl to my house. My flat was on the second floor and his family lived on the first floor.

Gathering enough courage one day I invited Swati to my home on a Sunday. I waited for her arrival nervously while watching TV. She came on time and observed the room closely when she entered the room.

"Oh. How dirty is your flat!" She exclaimed.

"I know," I said calmly.

"You don't know how to clean your flat. Have you noticed how clean our house is?" She went on about the cleanliness thing, I was least interested in.

"I am not interested in this cleaning talk. I am interested in something else," I said while pulling her hand towards me, sitting on the bed.

Now she was sitting on my bed with me holding her hands. I hold her face in my hands and kissed her on the forehead.

"It looks like you are missing me these days?" Swati said.

"I know you want to hear 'yes', but I will say nothing," I teased her.

We kissed on the lips. My head was reeling due to excitement. I pushed her down on the bed and started to feel her body.

I tried to remove her top. This time she felt less hesitation in removing her clothes, as there was no Mona to disturb us. Soon, both of us were lying on the bed, all naked. After exploring bodies of each other for some time we went all the way.

After making out, we dressed up and went to a neighborhood restaurant for lunch. The leisurely afternoon felt so good with her. Even the *aloo matar* and *tandoori roti* served there tasted good.

❑

Loss

I didn't want to live the rest of my life at the mercy of my bosses. I wanted to take control of my own life. I prepared couple of business plans and sent to potential investors after discussing them with Suraj.

One fateful morning, the moment I reached office, I got a call from Swati.

She was crying uncontrollably on phone.

"What's the matter? Why are you crying? Tell me," I said showing concern.

She was not in a condition to talk. She kept crying for two minutes before the call was disconnected. I tried to call her several times but there was a network issue.

I sat down on my chair with a cup of coffee in hand and lots of worries in the head.

Swati called me again. This time also she was crying.

"For God's sake, tell me what has happened before the call gets disconnected!" I almost shouted.

"My mother has expired," she said crying.

"Oh shit!" I felt my head was spinning.

"When? What happened to your mom?" I asked her.

"She was feeling pain in the abdomen for last two days. We thought it was a minor issue. We had showed her to a doctor yesterday. We still don't know the exact cause for the death. She left the world this morning," she said still crying. It was unsettling for her.

"It's so sad. I am coming in a couple of hours," I said. Giving solace to her was useless. The void couldn't be filled.

I took a leave from the office and reached her home. There was depressing atmosphere there. Many relatives had gathered there. All were mourning. Swati and her sister were weeping inconsolably. I wanted to hug her to make her feel good, but it was not done amid so many of relatives. I spent some time there and then returned with a heavy heart.

Swati kept mourning for an extended period. She took almost no food for five days after the demise of her mother. Amid her phone calls she would start talking about her mother and started crying. I tried my best to give her solace. She took more than three months to become normal.

A month later, I got a call from Mahesh. He was the guy sitting beside Shruti in my last company.

"Hi! Amit. How are you?" He asked.

"Hi! Mahesh, I'm just fine. How are the things at your end?" I asked out of courtesy.

He informed me about his mind-numbing monotonous work in a BPO in Bangalore.

Then he told me something I was not prepared for.

"Shruti is no more in the world!" He said with a sad tone.

"What?" I was shocked. I was left speechless for a minute. Memories of wonderful moments spent with Shruti suddenly flooded my mind.

"When? How?" I gathered my thoughts to ask.

"She was killed in a car accident yesterday. I was fired by Romila and was working in Bangalore for last one year. I was in touch with Shruti. I called you as you were her friend one time," he said.

"So sad." All I could say.

For the next couple of days, Shruti's memories kept clouding my mind. We shared a wonderful relationship. I thought she met me too late in her life. Otherwise we could have a life together. She lived in some corner of my heart. A mere mention of her name would make my day. We shared a great chemistry which was difficult to describe. I couldn't believe she was no more.

The death of Shruti made me aware of the short-lived nature of life. Some time back I was talking with her, laughing with her, walking with her and suddenly all gone forever. We need to value love, and value the person who is special to us.

The news of sudden demise of Shruti made my heart grow fonder for Swati.

Few days later I had a dream about Swati. I was with her in a large hall in a hill station. It was snowing outside. Some unseen power was forcing her away from me. She was calling my name and I kept on looking at her curiously. Slowly I realized she had gone away from me forever. I felt disturbed. I came out of the hall and searched for her for hours, sweating in the cold. At last I sat down on the white snowy ground holding my head in disappointment.

In the morning, I realized I might also lose Swati. I didn't want that to happen. Maybe it was the nature's way of telling me that I should hold on to her.

❑

A New Beginning

I and Suraj had a new business plan. It was related to the Internet industry. We had a plan to launch a shopping portal. Due to the growth of Internet users in the country the market was finally opening up for e-commerce in the country. Money was the only issue. My last efforts to raise funds were futile.

This time also a couple of investors invited me for chat, though didn't commit to invest money. One venture fund refused to give us funding, claiming Indians didn't shop online. The same investor gave money to an NRI for a similar business plan. My latest investment searching activity confirmed something I had already doubted – most of the investors were biased in favour of NRIs and those from IIM or IIT. It was a case of discrimination by the elite class against not-so-privileged Indians. College dropouts like Steve Jobs and Bill Gates should thank their stars that they were not born in India.

We realized that starting a new business required lots of balls. It was not easy and certainly not for the faint-hearted. We had to face several problems and financial uncertainly. This was not something the middle-class people prepare their kids for. We had to forego luxuries and live without usual trappings of a well paid job.

We prepared our minds to forego certainties of a 'settled life' for the unforeseen in the hope of having a big company of our own some day.

We decided to leave no stone unturned. We sent out hundreds of emails to all prospective investors and made calls to several of them. We knew venture funding was hard to come, but kept trying.

After months of efforts, one of Suraj's uncles agreed to invest some money in our venture. We collected our savings together for the required capital. I sold my bike to raise capital. Soon we had enough to start the venture full time.

We decided to resign from our full time jobs at Singhal's office. In a short span of time we got our company name registered, rented a new office and hired a couple of staff. It was a small step towards a long journey.

The last day at Singhal's office made me nostalgic. The memories of my first job came to my mind. How the boss of that company used to hire and fire in dozens; how he took the staff to a free trip to Mussoorie, where we had party on the night of 31st December; how the over-sized, round-shaped boss passed out at the dance floor after overdrinking, and it took four of us to carry him over to his hotel room.

I also got reminded of my second job. It was an immigration consultancy firm. The company boss Ajay Mehta hired a Mumbai-returned model as Chief Operating Officer. The ex-model had a failed modeling career but soon turned out to be an excellent actor. He was a smooth-talking incompetent rascal. He made it a habit of promising the moon to the customers. Soon, hundreds of well-educated Indians from all walks of life were promised to get visa and permanent residency of the UK, Canada, Australia or any country of their choice in just two months. The advertisements about the scheme were published in leading newspapers of the city. The company made a hefty amount in that scheme.

After three months we started to have so many queries from the customers desperate to go abroad. The model-turned-executive gave me the thankless jobs of handling customer complaints. I was flooded by questions of customers hoping for the next flight out of the country. A couple of female customers even resorted to flirting with me, hoping to get their work done faster. Some were describing to me how they had always dreamt of going to 'phoren' and supposedly I had the key to their dreamland. It was before the recession hit the global economy in 2008.

It was both embarrassing and amusing that hundreds of doctors, lawyers, nurses, chartered accountants, secretaries, and software engineers wanted to leave India as soon as possible, as if they were going to be burnt alive if they stayed here for even a day more.

I left the job after ten months. I used to get calls from those hopefuls even after two years.

It was a rollercoaster ride!

It felt so good to be finally our own boss!

The initial days of our venture were hectic. We tied up with distributors, courier companies and web solutions providers. We launched our shopping portal in a month. After marketing the portal for some days, we started to get orders from all parts of the country. We were selling a range of products like books, mobile phones, cameras and laptops.

Some days later, I heard an interesting piece of news.

Shantanu called me one day. "Hey Amit, you know what? Romila has been fired from the job!" He said. I was pleasantly surprised. It was a poetic justice that she got fired after firing a couple of staff of her office. The news was like a pleasant surprise. I felt very happy imagining her getting fired with humiliation, the way she fired me.

"Really? How come?" I asked Shantanu while trying to hide my happiness.

"The promoter's US-returned son has now taken over the operational department. He didn't like Romila and found her to be inefficient and manipulative," he said.

"Mansi must be sad at this turn of events?" I asked him.

"No. She surprised me yesterday by saying that she always hated Romila," Shantanu said. Mansi hating Romila? It was difficult to digest considering sisterly love they shared. Though, you never know the real feelings of a woman. You need to scratch many layers to see her true colours!

I felt like offering a job to Romila. Wouldn't be it a sweet revenge if I offered her a job and then fired her the same way she fired me, I thought.

❑

Social Pressure

One evening my father called me.

"So, have you decided to marry that girl?" He wanted to know.

"I will marry only Swati," came out of my mouth.

"Who? Swati!? Who is this girl?"

"She is my friend," I said.

"Is she a Brahmin?" He wanted to know.

"No. She belongs to some other caste.

"No. You can marry only a Brahmin girl. Our tradition does not allow inter-caste marriage. We carry huge social respect as a Brahmin family. You can't bring that to ground," he said.

The pride of the caste raised its ugly head. I felt most of my relatives did nothing with their lives, thinking being born into a Brahmin family was great enough. They used their caste name as an excuse for wasting their lives.

"The caste system is a social evil. I don't believe in that. I don't care about it. If I ever marry a girl it would be Swati. Otherwise I can stay bachelor forever," I explained in a firm but polite voice. It must have sounded *filmi* to him, I thought.

He didn't seem convinced and cut the call midway.

The next week my parents came to Delhi to brainwash me further. They tried to convince me to marry the girl of their choice. Besides cooking delicious food for me, my mother used her persuasive skills to the fullest.

I became a subject of intense brainwashing and emotional blackmail. But I stuck to my ground. I had finally decided to marry only Swati.

One day father got a phone call from one of my cousins. He looked worried while on the phone. I was in the same room.

"What's the news? You are looking worried?" Mother asked.

"Ramnath bhaiya has tried to commit suicide. He is in a hospital," father said. He was talking about Ramnath Mishra, the rich distant relative of us, who was running his firm in Lucknow.

"Oh. What happened?" Mother asked.

"His son has got married without informing him. After the wedding ceremony he called him to inform about it. Bhaiya couldn't take it. It was completely unexpected to him. So sad, he's struggling for life in the hospital," father lamented.

There was silence in the room for few minutes. It was ironical that my mother had once tried to make him and his children an epitome of the Indian culture, obviously without knowing his son well. The grass always looks greener on the other side, especially to lazy people.

One day I talked about the relative to Suraj.

"It's such a shame that supposedly social disrespect, illusion in most cases, causes even intelligent people to take such stupid and drastic measures," I said.

"There is a huge amount of pressure on people to follow traditions. The moment a man is born he is shackled in social bondage and expectations," he said.

"But it shouldn't make people take stupid decisions like done by Mishra uncle. He had almost everything an average people in our county wants. Obviously the desire to control children's life is so intense in the society," I said.

"Our society even today does not give much space to individuals. We try to follow social norms," he said.

"Who sets the social norms? It can be changed to suit the changing times. They can't be same as they were hundreds of years back. Do you know in my ancestral village there is a small temple of a *sati*, a woman who killed herself after the death of her husband. And all the village women worship her. I had seen it once myself in childhood. If people seriously want to follow the traditions then an illiterate man should not give good education to his kids, to keep up the tradition. They should stop using a mobile phone, as it was not used by our ancestors. Why follow traditions selectively and at your own convenience?" I said.

"It's difficult to explain. You won't understand it, as you are not a normal social person," Suraj said.

"What do you mean? I am not normal?" I asked him.

"I mean you are different. You don't do many things, supposedly done by normal people,"

"Well, in that case I am very happy the way I am," I said.

I felt as Suraj was forced to marry against his own wishes by his parents, now, he was finding ways to justify his capitulation to parents. Psychologically speaking, it would help him find peace with himself, I guessed. I hoped he wouldn't force his own sons and daughters to marry against their wishes.

Swati called me on a phone to fix a date. We decided to meet at our favourite, the Lodhi Garden. I noticed she looked weak due to the extended period of mourning the death of her mother. She had lost some weight too.

We sat on a bench enjoying the cloudy weather.

"You know what? May parents have come over here. They want me to marry a girl of their choice," I informed Swati.

"You are the only person in the world who understands me after my mother passed away. Sometimes I feel I am forcing you to marry me. I have decided not to do that. If you don't want to marry me, you can marry the girl chosen by your parents. I won't complain. But I will not marry anyone in that case. I have finally decided that," she said.

"You don't need to remain unmarried. A boy wants to marry you," I said.

"Who?" She asked.

"It's me," I said and hugged her tightly.

I could see a broad smile on her face.

"I have already told my parents that I will marry only Swati," I told her.

She looked speechless for few moments. Then looked into my eyes to get convinced.

"Today is the happiest day of my life," she said with a beaming smile.

Suddenly it started drizzling. We initially ignored it. Much to our surprise, heavy drizzling started to wet us. We stood up and decided to stand under a big tree. There was a big tin shed in the middle of the garden that could save us from rain. We decided not to go there as many people were already taking shelter there.

Soon it started raining heavily. The strong wind and heavy rains reduced visibility. We could not clearly see other people in the park. I realized we were going to be drenched in rain soon. I decided to take advantage of the situation. I hugged Swati and brought my face close to her. Then I kissed her passionately. It was a slow and wet kiss that lasted for long. One by one all our clothes started to get wet. Now we both were completely wet standing under the tree. The big tree could not save us from getting drenched from the head to the toe due to heavy rain and strong wind. We were standing under the tree touching and feeling wet bodies of each other. Swati was looking amazingly sensuous in that wet *salwar-kameez*. For me it was a unique experience. We kept kissing and feeling each other for nearly forty minutes till the rain was reduced to a light drizzle.

As our clothes were wet, we're feeling uncomfortable. We went straight to Nehru Place and went inside McDonald's to sip hot coffee for warmth.

❑

Shantanu's Troubles

One day I saw Shantanu Basu making an update on a social networking website about his visit to a local police station in Noida. I was curious to know why he needed to go there. When I called him he was busy in his office, He promised to talk to me in the evening.

When I didn't get the call in the evening I gave him a call the next day.

"Hey Shantanu. What's the matter?"I asked him.

"You know what? The Noida policemen are illiterate," he said with anger.

"What? I guess they maybe not," I reasoned.

"When I went to them to report an FIR they refused to accept it as it was written in English. They said it was Uttar Pradesh and they will accept FIR written in Hindi only. Those are fools. The problem is that I can't write in Hindi. I somehow solved the problem," he said.

"Ok. But why you needed to go to a police station?" I asked.

"Well, nothing much," he tried to hide the matter.

"Don't be so secretive. Relax. Be open with me," I assured him. .

"I had to file an FIR against my wife," said he.

"What? Against wife?" I was shocked this time.

"Yes. I am also going to file for divorce. My marriage can't work any longer. My wife is creating trouble and she tore apart many of my favourite books, just to hurt me. She had also complained to the police that I was harassing her," he said.

"What is the reason behind these all troubles?" I asked.

"She can't live with my parents. I had to choose between my parents and my wife. I have chosen my parents. We are soon going to live separately," he said. I could feel he was sad and disturbed at this strange turn of events. Only if I could help him some way!

"Why did you marry her in the first place?" I asked him, even though the question sounded unkind.

"My parents chose her as she belonged to our caste and our *kundlis* matched," he said.

"Can you marry a girl just because she belongs to you caste or due to *kundlis* matching?" I asked him.

"My parents forced me to marry her. Now they are also repenting. The new rings I wore on my left hand fingers didn't save my marriage. We even had a couple of *havans* at home, but they didn't work," he said.

"Do you really expect *havans* and rings to make your marriage work?" I asked him.

"Well, one of my cousins wears similar rings and he's leading a happily married life," Shantanu said.

"His marriage may be working due to their chemistry and compatibility, not due to some silly rings. One of my cousins also married after *kundli* and caste matching and like your case he also got divorced. Even thousands of brides, who are burnt by in-laws after marriage, are married only after *kundli* matching," I reasoned.

I was not shocked by the behaviour of Shantanu.

One evening I discussed the problem of Shantanu which he was facing, with Suraj.

"Suraj, I feel Shantanu is very superstitious. You know he married Pujita, his first wife, on advice of an astrologer. And he married his second wife as their *kundli* matched. How pathetic! One should marry someone due to love, compatibility or chemistry, not due to some stupid mumbo jumbo," I told Suraj.

"Well, he is also a part of the majority. Most people usually behave like him," he said.

"That's why we have so many godmen in the country, all making fool of people and making themselves richer day by day. All godmen are frauds and so are astrologers. I had read some days back that even some ISRO scientists believe in superstitions like astrology and palmistry. The problem lies with the education system of the country that gives importance to only passing exams, not developing critical thinking," I said.

"How can you say so? I know some astrologers who have some accurate predictions under their belt," he said.

"Most of the predictions prove to be false. Only a small number of them, that turn out to be true by chance, are remembered and publicized by these charlatans. All failed predictions are conveniently forgotten. It's all guesswork, no science," I said.

"If it's true then why the government is not banning astrologers for misleading people?" He asked.

"Because people running the government are superstitious themselves. They consult astrologers and seek guidance of godmen. You can't expect them to promote scientific and critical thinking in the country," I said.

"Even the media whose duty is to enlighten masses has been sold. Regional newspapers have regular astrology columns, while TV channels show sponsored programmes promoting various godmen," I added.

Suraj changed the topic soon. Looking at rings in his fingers I guessed he or his parents must be believing in magical powers of stones.

❑

Wedding and Tear Shedding

Swati informed the members of her family about my marriage decision. One day I got a call from her father.

"Hi Amit, how are you? I want to meet & talk to you in private," he said.

"I am fine, uncle. Is everything ok?" I asked.

"Can you please meet me some day? It's important. Can you come over to my office," he said.

"Sure. I will. Which day?"

"Come tomorrow," he said.

I noted down his office address and went to meet him. I was surprised why he called me to meet not at home, but the office. Maybe he wanted to talk to me in private.

He was standing at the reception of his office. I spotted him as his face was well described by Swati in the past. He was a tall and lean man with moustache and spectacles. He took me to a nearly coffee shop Barista. It was not crowded.

He ordered two cups of coffee.

"See son. I know about you, your family and your decision to marry my daughter. Swati has told me all," he said in a baritone. "My daughter wants to marry you as she likes you.

She has refused to marry anyone in the past. But before you decide to make her your life partner, I want to reveal something to you. I don't want to keep you in the dark. Some day you may know about it and may feel cheated," he continued.

"Ok. Let me know. You can trust me with a secret," I said calmly. I was suspicious he might say something unpleasant.

"Swati is not my biological daughter. Her mother worked in the administration department of a hospital. Swati's parents had abandoned her at birth. My wife adopted the baby. We have brought her up with lots of love and care, and have never let her know that we're not her biological parents. Only a handful of relatives know this," he said.

I was surprised, though not shocked. I felt sympathy for Swati and also felt good about the big heart of her late mother, full of motherly love and care for her kids. The abandonment was not surprising considering we were living in a country where female foeticide was rampant in some parts. It's just that about abandonment I had only read in newspapers or saw in movies. I personally knew no case till that date.

"You can trust me. This revelation only made me like Swati more. Her mother had such a big heart," I said.

"You promise me you won't reveal this ever to Swati," he requested.

"I promise I'll never do that. This is not a big deal for me. Who brings you up is more important that the biological parents. It doesn't really matter to me. Don't worry at all," I said firmly.

The old man looked relieved.

"So, Swati told me that you are facing resistance from your parents on marriage issue," he asked me, now looking more relaxed and confident.

"Yes. I have finally decided that I will marry Swati. However, my parents are opposing this as you belong to a different caste," I said sipping the hot coffee.

"I can understand your problem. I will give you my full support. If you want any help let me know. After death of my wife, I am really worried about marriage of my daughters. You never know for how many days I will live," he said.

"You are healthy. You'd live long. Don't feel that way," I tried to make him feel good.

"Yes. But you never know about life. Even her mother's death was completely unexpected," he said thinking about the past.

Soon he went to his office and I want back to my office. I could feel his care for his daughter.

Before returning to Gorakhpur, my parents decided to convince me once again for following their path. Mother decided to let me know about their decision.

"If you want to marry a girl of other caste then we will be forced to snap ties with you. We'll have nothing to do with you in that case," mother said.

"Who is forcing you to do that?" I was curious.

"Our society won't allow this. We will be socially boycotted by our relatives and people of the society," she said.

"Who will boycott you? Let me know. I will talk to all of them. It's not done. It's not the Middle Ages. We are living in a modern society. No one can do anything to you," I asserted.

"You don't know anything."

"Just give me their mobile numbers. I'll talk to them," I said.

"They won't invite us to their social occasions like marriage etc.," she said.

"Stop all this and just give me number of relatives who will boycott you," I said. I knew it was an excuse to convince me.

"Your young brothers won't be able to marry. No one will give daughters to our family," she said.

"Nothing like this happens anywhere. If the boy is doing a job then he will get married. Even jobless get married. Nothing will stop just because I marry a girl of my choice. If they face problems in finding a girl for marriage I will help in that case," I said.

'How dare you say so? We are here to help them get married. You don't have any role in that," she said with anger.

"I don't want to do any argument with you now. Just go and marry her. But you'll never see our faces," she said throwing a tantrum.

The next day parents went back to their home town.

It's difficult to fight with your own parents. You lose even if you win.

I met with Swati to describe what had happened between me and my parents.

"My parents are totally against my marriage with you," I told her.

"You should try to convince them more. They will agree after some time," she said.

"I don't know. I don't want to hurt them. I love them and care for them," I said.

"Can you give me your father's phone number?" She asked me.

"Why?" I asked.

"I want to say 'hi' to him." She said.

I gave her the mobile number of my father.

After a week, I got a call from father.

"What kind of girl is Swati? She called me and was talking about her marriage to you," he said angrily.

I was taken aback. "What was she saying?" I asked him.

"She said that we are pressurizing you to marry a girl of our caste. She sounds dominating. In the Indian society girls do not talk about their own marriage. It's parents who talk about marriage not sons and daughters," he said.

"Ok, in that case you can talk to Swati's father. He'll be glad to talk to you," I said.

"No. How can he talk to me? Won't he feel ashamed as he belongs to another caste? He should find a boy of his caste for his daughter," father said.

I finally understood that making my parents see my point was useless.

When I asked Swati, she admitted that she talked to my father about our marriage. There was nothing wrong about that, I felt. My father didn't take it in the right spirit as he had old ideas.

By now I was sure that my parents would not accept my marriage with Swati. We decided to marry nevertheless, encouraged by people's suggestions that parents would accept the relationship after the marriage. I wanted to keep it a secret affair. I didn't want my relatives to know about that as it would cause social embarrassment to my parents.

We had the wedding ceremony at Swati's house. I invited only Suraj and Shantanu Basu for the marriage. Most of Swati's relatives were present on the occasion. The ceremony was kept very simple. I kept on thinking about my parents and brothers during the entire ceremony conducted by a young *panditji*.

Swati came to my home after the wedding. She was excited about living with me, taking care of me, cooking for me and most importantly keeping the house clean. I never understood how cleaning a house can be exciting for a person!

After the marriage I called my parents.

"Please forgive me. I have married Swati. I can't live without her. Please accept our relationship now. I want to come over to you with Swati," I told my mother on phone. I thought my humility would do the trick.

"We have no relationship with you. Don't come here and don't call me again," my mother said and cut the phone call midway.

I was in tears. I could live without my parents but didn't want to. Swati also felt sorry for me. I didn't sleep the entire night, and kept thinking about my parents. I felt terribly bad that they had avoided contact with me for a stupid system like caste. Was society more important to them than their own son, I wondered. Maybe they refused to accept me because they had two other sons, I felt. I remembered the moments when I felt cared for by my parents.

May be they were ok as they had two more sons, but I was crying because I had only one mother and one father.

Slowly it became clear to me that I had paid a big price for marrying with Swati. I felt I would never be able to see parents. However, I was happy with Swati. She took good care of me. Though, no one could take place of your parents in your life.

❑

Six Months Later

One day Suraj informed me that our small company had won an award as a 'Best Startup of the Year', given by a leading organization promoting small businesses in India. It was a nice moment of recognition for us. Both of us had to go to Mumbai to receive the award in the next week. After months of slogging, the company was close to reach the point of breakeven.

I started feeling headache in the evening. While returning from the office, I purchased medicine for the headache. The moment I entered my house, I saw my father sitting in the room, while mother was helping out Swati in the kitchen. I was pleasantly surprised to see them and touched their feet, as per our tradition.

We didn't talk for few minutes. I was looking down. Mother now came out of the kitchen.

"Even if kids leave their parents, they will never leave their children," mother said. I wondered when I left them. It was ironical as they had left me, not the vice versa. I was no longer feeling headache.

They accepted our marriage now. After some days, they organized a reception programme in Gorakhpur. It was their way to show to the society that their son had married against their wishes but they finally accepted him.

❑❑❑